LOOKING AT THESE PICTURES I START WONDERING: how does a person show improvement with age? People say one matures with time, but how does it manifest? Does the energy in one's eyes change? Does one grow more considerate toward others? Does one show more humility? More self-control? Become more patriotic? As I age, will I become more patient and cultivate a loving attitude toward others? Will I become selfless? Will that really happen just because of age? I remember the day my high school principal retired. It was a particularly hot day and the sun was blazing. During the retirement ceremony the students were told to stand in an open field with no shade, while the principal, and only the principal, got an awning over his head. He went on and on about his accomplishments. People like to say teaching is selfless and noble, but he seemed pretty self-absorbed, oblivious to the students' wish for his speech to end so we could clap a bit and head back into the classroom. I don't even remember that oblivious asshole's name. What does it mean to become a "grown-up?" How does one go about doing that, growing up? Will I just become like my parents? I'd like to know if I can actually become a better person. Will I survive long enough to look back at my life and reflect on it fondly?

BLOOD SISTERS

Kim Yideum

TRANSLATED FROM THE KOREAN
BY JIYOON LEE

Deep Vellum Publishing
Dallas, Texas

Deep Vellum
3000 Commerce St., Dallas, Texas 75226
deepvellum.org · @deepvellum
Deep Vellum is a 501c3
nonprofit literary arts organization founded in 2013.

ISBN: 978-1-941920-77-0 (paperback) | 978-1-941920-78-7 (ebook)
LIBRARY OF CONGRESS CONTROL NUMBER: 2019937124

Blood Sisters is published under the support of
Literature Translation Institute of Korea (LTI Korea).

Text set in Bembo, a typeface modeled on typefaces cut by Francesco Griffo
for Aldo Manuzio's printing of *De Aetna* in 1495 in Venice.

Cover design by Anna Zylicz | annazylicz.com

Typesetting by Kirby Gann

Distributed by Consortium Book Sales & Distribution.

Printed in the United States of America on acid-free paper.

CONTENTS

Translator's Note

"You must care a lot about this novel to spend so much time with it," a new friend who had just learned about my translation project asked me. "What made you choose *Blood Sisters* for your project?" My answer at the time was something like this: translating this novel was an opportunity to create a productive conversation between two intertwined and porous cultural spheres: America of the late 2010s and Korea of the 1980s. Both spheres speak to struggles with mental health awareness, sexual violence, and hostile political climates. Also, describing and translating the Korean cultural practice of addressing each other by the role one plays ("teacher," "boss," "older brother," and so on) allowed me to meditate on how we as humans seem to encounter one another first through the role we play in each other's life with its accompanying expectations, and how puncturing the boundaries of those roles (dropping the honorifics and titles, falling in love) can be a precarious and daring act, a site of contact where desire, hatred, and identification take place.

In addition to those answers I'd like to share a personal reason for spending so much time with *Blood Sisters*. While translating *Blood Sisters*, I was going through major life events and my mental health was suffering. I witnessed Yeoul the protagonist struggle to navigate a hostile world with no parents, no mentor, and no reference point to give her direction, and I saw how art could become a hypnotizing space of projection where she could trace her own desires. I found myself engaging with the novel in a similar way. I projected my own past experiences—with depression and dissociation and my own negative inner dialogue—onto Yeoul's, and I experienced an intense identification with her and with a Korea that felt at once familiar and strange.

A few weeks before sending off the final version of the manuscript, while in Korea, I decided to go visit Kim Yideum at her recently opened bookstore-café in Ilsan, Café Yideum. Having lived in the United States for over fifteen years, as regretful as it is to say, Korea has become something of a foreign country to me: I don't know how to navigate it as I once did, and the food no longer sits as well. After a long, confusing bus ride with multiple transfers, I managed to meet up with Yideum at her Café Yideum, a cozy place brimming with a great selection of books. The posters for the reading series she hosts and a handwritten menu for teas perch on the wall, and a handwritten sign that says BOOK PHARMACY hangs on the doorway. When I asked her what a "book pharmacy" was she explained to me (while preparing some oolong tea) that upon request she "prescribes" a book for her customers after a conversation with them. In a way, I felt like *Blood Sisters* was the book Yideum Unni* prescribed for me, without either of us realizing. The novel asked me

---

* *Unni* is used to address a younger woman or an older sister.

the questions that I needed to be asking myself. I believe there is healing in being asked the right questions and meditating on the answers. Isn't that the reason why we are drawn to a particular work of art or particular people in the first place? Each encounter allows us to ask ourselves important questions and to search for their answers. On that note, I'm grateful to the books and the people who are close to me in my life. I hope you find in this novel the questions that you need someone to be asking you.

—Jiyoon Lee, April 2019

Part I

Blue Stockings

I open my eyes. I close them. *Shit. Goddamned sunshine.*
I squint and gaze at the blurry moving object before my
eyes. Wavering pale ankles. Long legs that keep extending.
And blooming buttocks . . . *Fuck! Let me see the whole you.*
My head is splitting apart. The woman is facing the window
askew; her brassiere is wrapped around her waistline, full
with two lovely rolls. She closes the hooks, turns the bra
around, and pulls it up to her breasts—her round, full, warm
breasts. Her face is hidden by her bushy hair. *Turn toward me.
Hold me! Kiss me!*

Throughout my life I've seen countless naked women's
bodies. Beautiful ones. Well, to be specific, I've seen hundreds of paintings of women's nudes. From Botticelli to
Courbet to Dali, all their female nudes. I've seen them all.
Realism, Surrealism, the year of completion, blah blah blah,
I don't really care. I just liked the ones reprinted in high res-
olution. One day in the corner of the silent library, I put my
tongue on the print of *L'Origine du Monde*. When I did that,
it felt like my body turned into wet foam, curling into itself,
sucked into that hole—leaving this filthy, noisy world, its
pop quizzes and minimum wage.

This live nude painting—here and now—is sensual in

her toasty peach-fuzz. "I would never have taken up painting if God didn't give women breasts in such marvelous ways." I recall Renoir said something like that, then painted his life away. I probably indulge in women's nudes as much as he did. It doesn't really matter whether I see the marvel of the cosmos or merely a voyeur's object.

The plaster casts for fine arts students that stood along my high school's corridor were always mottled in graffiti and dirt. As a member of the Fine Arts Club, I was in charge of cleaning them. It was an endless cycle: if I erased the beard off one face the night before, the very next morning a crotch would be covered in pubic hair, a chest covered with twenty nipples. "Lowbrows, they just don't get art," muttered the art teacher. He tenderly held the Venus he had sculpted himself, and sleazily slow danced his way into the art room. He shrouded her in a white veil, placed her in the corner of the drawing room, and then told me to lock the door behind me and to make sure to check the lock before I left.

The next day I just had to scream. Oh, Jesus, which one of you perverted motherfuckers crawled in here? Who knocked over our Venus and sprayed fucking semen everywhere? I tenderly wiped Venus's lips and throat with a rag for a while, but then threw the rag aside and stormed out. I thought about asking my friend to get my brushes and palette from the art room, but I didn't care anymore. That was it—I was done with the Fine Arts Club where I mostly killed time anyway.

"Keep pushing on as though you just started" was the motto given to the club, but mine was the polar opposite.

I never finished anything. It was easier to erase it and start over. Easier than swatting a fly.

There she is between my half-closed lids. "Are you awake?" Jimin Sunbe[1] is asking. "I'm gonna be late again." Brassiere fastened, her form clothed. "See you later!"

"Wait a sec!" I start coughing. I want to say I'm sorry, I want to say I went over the line last night, but the door slams shut. *What's the occasion? She's putting on a skirt? And even lipstick?* Ever since I started crashing at her place, Jimin Sunbe's outfit was consistent. She always had her hair tied in a tight ponytail, wore a T-shirt and a pair of jeans, and threw on a black jacket and gray scarf. When she added her giant backpack, she looked like a traveler about to go on a trip.

Last night, Jimin, without warning, led a woman with an outfit similar to hers and two men into the room. I was just splitting the hard ramen noodles in half to throw them into a pot of boiling water. *I didn't know we were having guests. Awkward.* I crushed the ramen with my fist.

"Say hello, everyone! Here are my dear friends, and this is . . . well, I've talked to you guys about her. This is a talent who hopefully will join our Blue Stockings Club." Jimin tapped my shoulder as she smiled—her pink chewing gum emerged between her lips. This was the first time I'd even heard of the Blue Stockings Club or anything about me

---

1. *Sunbe* is a term used by underclassmen to address older students. In Korea, it's expected to address others in terms of their social relationship to you, with names for upperclassmen, boss, older brother, younger sister, etc.

joining it, so I was mostly confused. I turned the stove off and bowed my head to the guests. My big toenails were blue (and they weren't the only things on my body that were bruised). The woman with a mole on her nose added more water and two more ramen packets into the pot. When she noticed the crushed smithereens of my ramen noodles, she abruptly blurted out, "So, are you and Jimin dating? Just kidding!" and cracked an egg into the pot. My ears felt hot.

We set up the foldable table to eat ramen together, but one guy said he'd already eaten and instead of joining us opened a book on the floor, and started rambling away. Words like "gender," "sexual minority," "social class," "proletariat," and "anarchists" were being thrown around. I couldn't swallow any of it—not the ramen, nor the kimchi, but especially not these words that felt heavy like lead candies. *Fucking hell. I hate these pretentious intellectual types. It's gonna be rough if they talk like this all day.*

"So, like, I have a . . . previous commitment. Goodbye."

"What? Where are you going in the middle of the night? You have nowhere to go," Jimin asked, perplexed.

I picked up my jacket anyway and fled the room. Picking at the crumpled heel of my shoe with my finger, I tried to think of a place I could go. I had nowhere, it was true. I felt lost.

I was squatting by the corner of the narrow alley for about thirty minutes when I saw a black cat with a perky tail walking along the brick fence. I meowed at him, but this Monsieur White Whiskers ignored me and kept going. I threw a pebble at him. After a while teenagers, probably middle schoolers, entered the alley. They were staggering and looked drunk. They were about to light their cigarettes, leaning against the fence, when their eyes met the pair of eyes belonging to a squirming heap in the darkness—me. They slowly backed away, tripping over trash cans, and ran out of the alley. *Assholes, I wasn't gonna bite.* I swear I am not hostile-looking, nor am I the kind of trash who mugs children. I'm just a defeated youth, a scream, a lamentation thrust into the sky. I enjoy my excellent loser attitude. The squirming heap in the darkness whispered into my ear: *You coward. What are you afraid of? Go on. Destroy yourself. You have the right to self-destruct.* Good thing I wasn't naive enough to be persuaded by nonsense like "a right to dream" or "a right to self-destruct."

Arf arf arf. A dog emerged. Was today the Thursday when all the dogs and cats on this earth hang out together? I doubt it was God dropping him on my lap. Probably a UFO threw this dog out along the way. Holding the ugly dog, I walked out of the alley, into the street. The street felt warmer. The main street was brimming with people.

I kept walking mindlessly. I found myself walking along the exact trajectory of the bus line heading toward my parents' home. I don't know about my father and stepmother . . . no, those *fuckers*, but I should've kissed my cat goodbye when I ran away from home. I didn't know things were going to get this bad when I first left. My cat probably threw a tantrum to get them to bring me back, probably went on a fasting protest. But by now she would be purring, comfy in my dad's crotch. My cat, Leche. When I would call *Leche!* she would run toward me. She would lap up milk—funny, Leche lapping up *leche*—the way she licked her jet-black paws. My calculating, lazy, petulant creature. I missed her.

I stopped in front of the pet shop. A shopgirl about my age opened the glass door to pull down the metal shutter. Her thighs were bulging out of her short leather skirt. She scowled at her nails. Her manicure must have been ruined. I approached the shopgirl, and showed her the stray dog I'd been carrying.

"Do you guys buy dogs by any chance? How much can you give me for this?"

"Wait, this isn't your dog! That's Nana. Her mama was looking everywhere for her!"

She told me Nana's mama was at some café right now. She painstakingly described the café, which turned out to be super easy to find. It would have been simpler if she just said the café was on the second floor of the building across from the Farmer's Coalition market, on the street that connects the university to the subway station. The interior of the café was dark and stuffy. *The first snow is falling*, the song that won some collegiate composer's award, was playing. It didn't suit the stale space. *Don't be sad, the white snow, the first one of this season, is falling.* I liked the song's opening; I'd spent my senior year of high school singing this song. It didn't snow then, however.

The café's owner yelped when she saw the dog in my arms, and started screeching, tears pouring out of her eyes. "Oh my god, where have you been, Nana? What happened? Did you get hurt, my love? Oh my baby, you must be starving!" She showered the dog with tender words I've never heard directed toward myself in my entire life. For a long time, the café owner was hysterical, but she finally got it together enough to bring up the words I was waiting for.

"How can I thank you? How can I reward you for bringing my Nana home?"

"Well, I wasn't really looking for a reward . . ." I coyly trailed off like I was some sort of kind animal rescue volunteer. I couldn't tell her what I was really thinking, not to her face, comically mottled with mascara. I hoped she'd just give me some cash and let me go, but she kept on asking what my name was, where I lived, what I was majoring in, all while her eyes were rapidly examining me up and down.

"Okay, okay. What do you think about working here? It doesn't matter if you have no experience as a server." She trailed off, watching for my reaction. "This is such a fortuitous situation, I will pay you a better rate."

Instant Days

I drank too much with the café owner that night. When I got back to Jimin's place there was no one there. The room was a mess. It looked like the secret police had raided the place. The chairs were toppled over among beer bottles, and books, notes, and pamphlets were strewn about everywhere. I zigzagged left and right to clean up the place. A little later, Jimin was back and explained that there had been an argument among her friends, but they eventually stopped fighting out of consideration for her. She'd just seen them off. I drank from one of the open bottles and curtly asked why they had to do the group study here. I shouldn't have said it, I was just a freeloader who wasn't paying rent or buying groceries—not even a single ramen packet—just hanging out for over two weeks now, a full moon cycle. I added further insult by telling her about my new job.

"You don't need to work at a shady place like that," she scolded. "I never asked you to pay rent. What was the point of running away from home if you were just going to walk right back into another shithole. It would be better to starve."

"You don't know anything about me!"

"You're being irresponsible! Think about it. What year

are you living in? You just stroll through campus, molotovs and tear gas in the air, and you don't feel anything?"

"Yup! I'm a clueless airhead. So what? Am I supposed to be like you, memorizing manifestoes and communist curricula, breaking bricks to throw at cops during a strike?"

"Think about the summer we met!"

"Fucking hell, I'm so tired of that story. We just protested because everybody was doing it! Everybody was protesting General Park's constitutional amendment, yelling catchy slogans, because how could we not? If you didn't join the protest, everybody would've thought you were an unpatriotic government dog! It's different now. I just protested because I wanted you to like me. I have no political ideology of my own. Don't tell me to read this book, that book, join your 'group study' like it's some sort of holy ritual."

"You've changed since your stepbrother died."

That's when all of the evening's drinks rushed back into my mouth. I ran to the shared bathroom down the hall with my hand over my mouth, but someone had locked the door. I puked all over the bathroom door. Someone emerged to curse me out. By the time I cleaned myself up, he was gone. I had no one to curse at, so I just lifted my middle finger to the sky. Fuck you, motherfucker. Godfucker.

I came back to the room to lie down, still huffing with anger. Jimin held my hand under the covers. Her fingers were raw from her blood-drawing nail-biting habit. We knew we had drawn blood from each other's hearts with our drunken argument, so we waited to fall asleep holding hands. She usually wrote before going to bed under the nightlight, but not tonight. Around dawn, we kissed. I held back my morning breath as our lips touched. I fell back to sleep.

Now I am putting away the futon and folding the pajamas she left behind. The room feels empty. I feel abandoned. I press the play button of the dusty cassette tape player. "A Bird on a Metal Tower" by Kim Dusu rings out of it. It's the tape I gave Jimin for her birthday. So she had listened. I thought she only paid attention to Kim Min-ki and Nochatsa.

I open the photocopy of Kim Nam-jo's poetry collection Jimin had given me. The very first page has an inscription: "Let's go forward together," in red, signed, "From, Warrior Jimin." Warrior, huh? She isn't as strong as she pretends to be. I usually don't like the poems Jimin likes. Same with the prose.

Mayakovsky isn't too bad. I like "A Few Words About Myself," "Cloud in Trousers." I heard he was a revolutionary, but his poems are avant-garde. I don't know poetry too well, but I don't want to know poetry too well. *I'm gonna read one more poem, take a shower, and head out.* I open the book carefully, like an illiterate shaman carefully picking a card. The title is great: "I Love."

I can't do it alone—
    carry the grand piano
(much less
a metal safe)
    Then how am I supposed to bring back this—

heavier than the grand piano
   or metal safe—heart of mine?
 Bankers are wise:
"We're unimaginably rich.
 We didn't have enough pockets
   so we stuffed our safes."
 I have hidden
   my love
   inside you
 like the riches
 in the safe
and like a Greek king
   I strut.

The entire poem is long, 13 pages total. They are aligned weirdly, texts too close to one another. I wonder if the photocopier messed it up? The indentation of the lines moves in and out, and the text size is inconsistent. After reciting on my own, I feel deflated and a little embarrassed. My heart gets heavier than a metal safe.

It's time for me to go to school, so I hurry out, leaving a note on the desk.

Jimin, If you have time this evening, stop by at the café where I work. It's on the way to the subway station, and it's called Instant Paradise. Sometime between 6:30 and midnight. Don't wait for me, they said they will feed me tonight. Enjoy your evening.

—Jeong Yeoul

★ ★ ★

This isn't commuting, this is mountain climbing! The stupid college gobbles up our tuition, but can't spit out a single shuttle bus for the students. Getting to the Humanities building isn't too bad, though. I have a German Grammar class at 4:00 PM. I've skipped too many classes and am not sure I'll keep going. I still haven't turned in the paper for my Interpreting Literature class. Ah, my heart is not a safe full of love, but a shriveled organ rotting with anxiety and anger.

I walk by the café where I now work. Instant Paradise. I salivate at the thought of a free dinner. The sign is already lit. I hadn't noticed, but the huge, hot-pink sign looks tacky and a little suggestive. Instant coffee, instant ramen, instant camera—what else is "instant?" My life? My disposable instant life! There is no past, no future; there is no previous life or reincarnation; there is no eternity. Just one disposable day after another, and then—GAME OVER! I wish life was made of a single day: today.

Jeong Yeoul! Let's not get distracted by the past nightmares, or make any foolish long-term plans. Here and now. Today alone is overwhelming enough. A black plastic bag soars above my head. It's majestic, like a raven midflight.

14

Zarathustra

It's been a week since I started working at Instant Paradise, but Jimin hasn't stopped by, not once. I know she is busy studying and writing poems, but it stings. When I get to her place after midnight, exhausted after a long day of work, she looks over her shoulder, avoiding me like I'm a pathetic prostitute. The past few days, she's stopped nagging me. *Stop working at that shady café. Read books.*

But the café is near the university, so there are almost no shady customers. Most of the customers are college students. Occasionally school teachers, bank clerks, or middle-aged men from the apartment complex across the street stop by. The owner shows up once every few days to ask half-heartedly, "Everything good? Water the plants, please." Then she scatters her perfume smell and storms out. According to her nephew and cashier, Sungyun, she also has a huge coffee shop in Gwangan, so she doesn't really care about this location. Her father owns the building, and she has good alimony from her divorce, so she isn't really worried about money.

I am just about to brush my teeth after eating dinner in the kitchen when a tall man shambles into the shop. The sign's light is off and it's ten minutes before the store opens for the evening.

"Excuse me, we're not open yet." I look up, and my heart drops. *Oh fuck, it's Dad.* He probably poked around the university student directory office, somehow heard about Jimin, and combed through the map to find her place. I can visualize him huffing and puffing through the university's gate, the flower shop, the convenience store, the real estate agent's office, and into the dark alley where Jimin and I live. He might have throttled Jimin to tell him where I was.

"I'm sorry, but can I use the bathroom?"

"What?" My father instantly transformed into a stranger. It wasn't him. I feel deflated, so deflated that I fall to the floor. Eunyong, another server, tells him that the bathroom is up the stairs halfway to the next floor.

How long has it been since the last time I saw my father face-to-face? It feels like it's been a million years since we ate at the same table. There is no way he has been thinking of me or looking for me.

The only time my father and I touched skin to skin was when I was in second grade. It was in the small, noisy work-shop attached to our home where my father made squishy slippers out of plastic. I kept playing the rubber band game, where you dance along to a song with a specific sequence of moves, jumping over a long rubber band set up high off the ground. When I wore a cumbersome skirt, I would pull up the skirt and tuck it in my panties so I could freely kick my legs as high as the sky.

One sweltering summer night, I saw my mom in a dream. She spread her arms toward me by the lake. I ran to her, my feet so light, to jump into her arms. But her breasts were as cold as ice. She was made of plastic. When I woke up, soaked in sweat, no one was there. Half-asleep, I played the rubber band game in the dark. There was no rubber band, so I piled up the pillows. I sang a familiar song to myself: "Hopping over the dead bodies of my fellow soldiers, I go forward and forward," and hopped back and forth over the pillows. But then I slipped on one of the pillows and bumped my head on the corner of the nearby desk. Blood spilled from my forehead. Covered in blood, I crawled into the workshop's control room. Dad, working late that night, turned pale at the sight of me, picked me up, and rushed to the hospital. His white undershirt quickly turned red. It was a sweltering summer night, but my teeth were chattering. I felt like I was freezing to death. I was so sleepy. And I felt so good. When we were passing the overpass by the public bathhouse, I prayed: *I hope the hospital light I see is farther away than it looks. Dear God, please let this overpass collapse.*

So now I have a scar on my forehead. I usually cover it with my bangs, but when I feel like shit, I trace the scar, slender like an orchid's leaf, and retreat into my heart's garden. In the garden there are trees, songbirds, rose bushes, pots of orchids, and pretty pebbles. A white bird emerges out of a pretty pebble. On the green grass, I drink hot cocoa, and a nude woman sitting next to me touches my cheek. *Who is my real mother?*

The man returns from the bathroom and asks if he could order an apple mojito. I don't know what that is. When I squint and tell him we don't serve food, he smiles, "But an apple mojito isn't food," and orders a gin and tonic instead.

I can make a gin and tonic with my eyes closed.

"Do you want a drink?" He doesn't even touch the shrimp chips that come with the drink. He orders another drink, the same one. There are five or six toothbrushes sticking out of his rat-colored pocket. He must be a toothbrush salesperson. Is he one of those people who loudly profess how amazing the toothbrush is that they're selling on the subway, trying to coax the passengers into buying one? He glances at the check and gives me twenty thousand won.

"The total is ten thousand." As I return one of the two ten thousands bills, he pushes it back into my hand. "Why would I take this?" I get annoyed, but Eunyong pokes my side to take it. *Oh, I guess this is what they call a tip.*

* * *

The Aesthetic Studies professor stops by. He studied Aesthetics at a prestigious university in Seoul. Now that I work at a café, I see people like this up close. I have to hide my excitement when I see him walk in with his fellow professors. I used to sneak into his class because everybody talked about him: he was a true believer in democracy, a great agitator, and a blindingly handsome man. I used to go all the way down to the Fine Arts wing of the university for his lecture, and I learned a few things about Lukács' philosophy among the slacker Dance majors.

When the party he's having with his friends warms up, the professor sneaks his arm around Eunyong. *Is that okay? He's allowed to grope her, just like that? Wait, should I have been sitting next to him?* I don't know how I feel about the situation. My head spins.

The professor's friend picks up a fork and moves his hand off my thigh. He sings into the fork as though it's a microphone. He sings a new pop song. His voice sounds like he is scratching the plate with a fork. I like the psychedelic song by Sanulim he's singing, but he's not getting it right, not even close. A professor next to him butchers Songolmae's "I Lived in Oblivion."

"Hey, you over there! You should sing a song," the Aesthetic Studies professor yells at me, and I decide to obey his command, but can't think of any song I know the lyrics to. I remember melodies better than lyrics. Everybody in the café is getting impatient with me. Whatever. I'll sing a song that will elicit applause for sure.

"Having endured the long night, like the morning dew on the grass leaves, more beautiful than a pearl, the sun rises above the cemetery, and the sweltering daylight torments me . . ." The song is reaching its climax, and I feel great.

"Hey! What the fuck. Stop that!" someone yells at me. The room quickly cools in silence. They all look angry, abruptly sobered up. "I don't believe this. You're just bargirls at a shitty bar, okay? I don't know what you think you know, but how could you sing a protest song here? Some things are sacred!"

After that everybody leaves, even the couple who have been giggling over two cups of coffee for several hours. Eunyong, Sungyun, and I go outside to talk. The two of them, who have worked here for a while, tell me that the tips are pooled and then split. But since it's my first time getting a tip, I get to keep it. I head to the record store by the university. There's a record I've been eyeing. *I hope it'sn't sold already.* I'm nervous. The album cover was beautiful, and the title was glorious. The cover art had a monster's face with diseased skin and an expressionless man caged inside its mouth. The man is probably the lead singer of the band. They are an Italian art-rock band called Museo Rosenbach, and the album is called *Zarathustra.* After all those days pressing my face against the display case window, peering at the album, I finally get to own it.

The dark and stuffy café is now filled with the fantastic *Zarathustra.* Running time: twenty-something minutes. I could listen to this album at least ten times a day, every day from now on.

"Are you just gonna play this record over and over again? I feel like I'm going insane listening to this!"

As Eunyong complains, I narrate, "Behold, I teach you, Übermensch. Man is something that shall be overcome!"

"You're acting like an intellectual buffoon." Sungyun replaces *Zarathustra* with Lee Guanjo's record on the turntable. "The customer is king. We need to play songs that they like." Sungyun is supposed to be majoring in Athletics, but he doesn't look it. He hangs out with the jocks in town who call each other "brother," but he's barely taller than me, maybe 175 centimeters. Sporting a buzzcut and wide shoulders, he boasts that he only wears brand-name sportswear and trainers.

"I'll donate the record here, since I bought it with the tip that should've been shared," I suggest.

★ ★ ★

Down the dark alley, I return to Jimin's place, swinging the plastic bag containing a pork cutlet I saved for dinner. The room is dark and quiet. "Jimin, are you asleep?" Nobody is there. She never stays out this late. Without washing my hands or anything, I just lie down on my belly, and open a book, *Thus Spoke Zarathustra*, one of the books Jimin begged me to read. I was probably drawn to Museo Rosenbach, not a very well-known band around here, because of her recommending this book. *Goddamn, this book is thick.* She would grin if she saw me struggling with it. *Where is she?* On the back cover, there is this passage: "The Earth has skin, and the skin is riddled with several diseases. One of the diseases is Man." After turning a few pages, I am overwhelmed by sleepiness and worry about Jimin's whereabouts. I can't help it. I can't help being the squirming skin disease. Even if the whole Earth self-destructs tomorrow, I'll just pull a blanket over myself. I'm the Sleepy Demagogue.

Aldebaran

Lately, Jimin Sunbe seems to be plotting something with other Sunbes. Jimin spent the past four days protesting at the day-and-night nonstop rally after the activist Lee Hanyeol passed away. She's that kind of bleeding heart. She resigned as the PR manager of the Feminist Students' Association group to go join the laborers at the Guro workshop. She gave up on that mission after her mom threw a fit, but she's still a troublemaker, big time. For some reason, she tries to embrace all the illnesses of the world with her bleeding heart.

During finals week, I never see Jimin come back to the apartment. She says she's been studying late at the library and in the activity room, but I don't know if she's even taking the exams or eating enough. She won't answer me when I ask what she's been up to, or if she does, the answer is curt. I want to hassle her into telling me what's going on, but I can't. I'm close to academic suspension myself. I turn in my German Grammar exam with almost nothing filled out, and the professor rejects my late paper. The electives aren't too bad, but even in those, I'm not sure what kind of grades I'll receive.

★ ★ ★

At Instant Paradise, the owner seems to have taken to me, so she doesn't care if I don't come to work during finals. She even copied the key to the café for me to keep, telling me to feel free to come study there. Tonight she's standing on the street with Nana in her arms.

"The stars are beautiful tonight," she says. I look up into the sky. When I walk, I only look down at the ground. Frankly, I find the people who ramble about the stars pathetic.

"I don't see any."

"You have to envision them through your imagination. One star, two stars, three stars."

There are too many of these romantic literary types in the world. I walk into the café, and she follows me.

"Yeoul, what's your zodiac sign?"

I'm getting real sick of this shit. "I was born in May, so probably Taurus."

"Hmm. You were born under the influence of Aldebaran. It's a large star, and in astrology, it's the star that brings fortune."

"Hmm. I guess that's nice." I find it strange how chummy she's being with me tonight. I wonder if she wants something from me. "Aren't you busy today? You usually are."

"Not today. By the way, did you know that you're popular here? Someone was looking for you."

"Me? Who was it?" I ask, intrigued.

"I dunno. We talked a little over drinks. I think he runs a hospital over in Gupo."

"I don't know anyone like that. He must've been looking for someone else."

"Sure. You need to get your tuition for the next semester ready, right? I'll pay you in advance so you can go buy some pretty clothes. You're wearing the same clothes all the time. When do you even wash them?"

Embarrassed, I mumble that I haven't eaten yet, so I need to get some food. In the kitchen, Eunyong whispers to me.

"Yeoul, she's trying to take you to her bar in Gwang-an. Be careful. Once you start working there, you can't really leave . . . There was another woman who worked here and left to work at that bar, and she . . . changed."

"What kept the café owner from taking you there?"

"I like it here. Sungyun Oppa[2] is nice to me. And I'm still a high school senior—a super senior at that. The customers at the bars prefer college girls. I'm not that pretty anyway."

"Super senior would imply you're actually prepping for the college entrance exam. I haven't seen you crack a book once."

"What, you think I like living like this? My mom says I don't need to go to college anyway. I'm just going to get married after making some nest egg money."

Eunyong and I make bibimbop in the kitchen. We mix the rice, bellflower roots, bean sprouts, some greens, and chili paste. The owner's mom often cooks for us and sends the food to us via Sungyun. Sometimes she sends something

2. *Oppa* is a term used to address an older brother and is also a term of endearment women sometimes use to address an older man.

24

simple. Rice, soup, and kimchi. Sometimes she sends marinated beef. She must be feeding us so that we'll work hard at her daughter's café. It's fine when she doesn't send us anything, we just cook ourselves ramen or pork cutlets, or order Chinese. Mothers seem to be their daughters' guardian angels or their enemies, there is no middle ground.

It's time to close the café, but the toothbrush salesman walks in. His hair is wet. It must be raining outside. We were ready to close so we all stand awkwardly.

"Come over here and eat some of this." The toothbrush salesman puts a big cake box on the table. We are all hungry. Sungyun appears out of nowhere and starts eating the cake with his hands. After scarfing down the entire cake, we remember to thank him.

The toothbrush salesman notices the music in the café. "Wait, you're listening to *Zarathustra*?!"

"You know this band? Yeoul said she's the only one who knows them!" Eunyong sticks her tongue out and calls me a liar.

"Your name is Yeoul? What's your last name? I came here to see you the other day, but you weren't here. I asked the owner about you." As I examine him, I realize that he reminds me of the photograph of my father when he was young: his pupils float in the upper side of the whites, the bridge of his nose is well defined, and the corners of his mouth are turned upward. "I should introduce myself first. My name is Han Jihyun. I live nearby, so I hang out around here."

★ ★ ★

I walk back home. I think of the café owner's remark. Aldebaran, schmaldebaran. There's not a single star to be seen, not even the moon can be seen in the sky tonight. I preferred the mandatory study halls, and nights I spent questioning what the point of my life even was, over working this pointless part-time job. I received my paycheck today, but I didn't even open the envelope. It doesn't feel like the hard-earned *fruits of my labor*. But maybe I'm overthinking all this, too influenced by Jimin's Marxist ideology.

On the sidewalk, I'm waiting for the light to turn green when someone slaps my back. I turn around to find my high-school friend.

"Oh my God! Is that you, Hyunmi?"

"Yeah! You look just the same."

"I thought you had gone to study abroad in America."

"No, my visa for America took too long to be processed, so I had to postpone my departure. I was actually going home after my going-away party with friends just now. I've been wondering what you're up to. Miryong and Eunsook said they both tried to contact you for the party, but . . . what's wrong with your stepmother? She cussed at them like a crazy person. I thought I wasn't going to see you before I left. Let's go somewhere and catch up."

Blue Moon

We head back to Instant Paradise. We walk a little apart from each other, giggling sporadically. I didn't know I was going to use the key to the café other than to lock up the place. There is some light coming out of the café. Strange, it should be closed. I push the key into the lock. *Click*, I get an inexplicable bad feeling in my gut.

"Hyunmi, don't come in. Wait out here." I slowly and quietly open the worn door to the café; the cobalt-blue paint is scratched off here and there. When I look inside, I notice a tipped-over backpack, Geography and Ethics text-books spilling out of it.

In the back corner near the DJ booth no one uses, the glaring butcher shop lighting is cast on Sungyun. His sweat-pants are at his ankles, he's leaning forward, his glutes flexed, looking like hunks of meat. He's holding his penis like a pole made of meat. A girl with her black skirt pulled up to her chin is lying before him, her exposed lower body writhing. I place my hand over my mouth, start to close the door, and Sungyun turns toward me. Did he see that it was me? I feel his pupils tremble like the needle of the butcher shop scale weighing a cut of pork.

I grab Hyunmi's hand, my face feels cold, and we run

down the stairs. Hyunmi suggests going to her car. The fume of her hot breath spills out of her mouth. We get into her car, and I lean into the seat. My head feels as foggy as the windshield.

"Yeoul, let's go see the sea."

I don't respond.

"Let's go see the nighttime beach, go for a walk. I know it's cold but it will be nice, no?"

"No thanks. I don't feel like it."

"Do you want the radio on?"

"No."

Hyunmi pouts. "We haven't seen each other for a long time, and like a miracle, we ran into each other. So why are you sullen? Aren't you happy to see me? Don't you know how much I liked you? Remember all the snacks, bento boxes, gifts, letters I gave you?" She chatters on.

Back when we felt constantly and desperately in need of something, feeling unfulfilled and underdeveloped, when we felt like we were going to go crazy unless we immersed ourselves in something, she acted as though I was a boy that she liked. She pulled me in by my neck, tearing up on the bench in the school garden. In the night time under the magnolia tree, she begged me to put my finger into her pussy. She didn't like that I had other friends and tried to keep me from going to the school snack bar with them. She followed me around, keeping me from going to the Fine Arts Club room. I found her irritating, but I never could refuse her lips that tasted like cherry candies.

•

Hyunmi lifts her head from the steering wheel to lean into me. I feel her earlobes against my neck. Her cheeks are wet and warm. She takes off her pearl earrings, and unbuttons her blouse. She moves over to straddle me, and kisses me lightly. She pushes her pale, firm breasts against my face.

"Please, suck me."

"I don't really feel like it."

"This is the last time we'll be together. This one last time."

Okay, this will be the last time I'll see you. So I'll do what pleases you. In this heated moment, I feel like I understand her, even love her. Such confusing sensations. Our lonely connection. Our heated breath. Condensation drips down the window. I wish for the car to fly across the night sky into an alien world a million miles away, to travel through a dark nebula, never to return.

Virus Complex

I turn in the leave of absence form, so a long break is ahead of me. School break, *banghak,* letting go of the learning. Does it always feel this light when we let go of the things we've been holding on to? I walk quickly across the campus, blowing on my cold hands to warm them. I suddenly feel melancholy, thinking that I might not be able to see all this again—the school library as warm as a greenhouse, the frozen winter trees on campus. I watch the small creek that winds through campus. The cold wind cuts through my body. I've been wearing this thin reversible coat the past few months.

A while back I stopped at my dad's place to pick up some of my winter clothes, but he changed the lock, so I couldn't get in. I kicked and shook the door, but it didn't budge. A boy, the son of the renters next door, said hello. He kicked the soccer ball over, so we passed the ball back and forth for a little bit, but I eventually turned around to leave, feeling defeated, my hands in my pockets. The boy must have wanted to continue; he stood in front of me to keep me from leaving. I looked at the soccer ball and its crooked shadow. I ruffled the boy's hair and forced a smile.

I walk into the alley and a scooter almost hits me. *Bitch!*

The man on the scooter spits on the ground, and starts the engine again. With a metal delivery case on the back, he speeds away like he's racing someone. I doubt his shitty scooter can keep up with the speed of his yearning.

When I get into the apartment, Jimin Sunbe is eating sweet and sour pork as though she's been starved, her face half-buried in the bowl.

"It's so unlike you to order this expensive dish!" I sit next to Jimin and split the wooden chopsticks, and she runs to the sink and vomits.

"Yeoul, don't you smell mugwort incense from this? It's foul."

"I haven't started eating yet, so I don't know."

"I ordered it because I was craving it, but now I can't eat it."

I finish the sweet and sour pork, and watch Jimin lying on her side. Her eyes are swollen, and her skin looks rough under the bright light. "Sunbe, come sit over here. I wanna draw you." Jimin smiles. Even when I showed off my pay-check, or got into a handstand and circled the room with my belly button showing, she didn't smile. Even when I told her I finally finished *Thus Spoke Zarathustra* like she asked me to, and even when I told her I liked her poems she didn't smile, but here she is, smiling slightly. It's been a long time since I saw her pretty pink gums. On the back of the page ripped from the calendar, the last month of the year, I draw her. The face that aches, the lovely face slowly building on the white space. The pencil keeps slipping off the slippery paper. I feel like I am ruining her beautiful smile with my terrible draw-ing. Should I stop here and leave it unfinished?

"I went to the café the other day." The smile disappears and her face is filled with grief. She always looks so serious. It scares off some of the underclassmen from approaching her, but she doesn't know that.

"Oh yeah? When was that? Why didn't you come in to say hi?"

"I . . . It was last month. I went there around midnight, because I know that's when you're usually done with work. The person who was there told me you stepped out briefly, and invited me to wait for you inside. He offered me a drink . . . You didn't come back. You must've gone home by then."

"Hmm. Was this person a man or a woman?"

"A man."

"That must be Sungyun. Why didn't he say anything to me?" Jimin says she's tired and lies down. She turns toward the wall. Her shoulders seem to tremble. Is she crying?

★ ★ ★

I don't want to go to Instant Paradise. I hate Instant Paradise. I swing the door open, thinking about quitting. I'm not really late, but Eunyong chastises me, "What took you so long?" An unfamiliar girl in a school uniform politely bows.

"You have something other than the school outfit, right? Get changed and wipe down the tables," Eunyong tells her, then explains that the café owner hired another part-time employee because it's summer, and when school is out we get more customers.

"But a high schooler?"

"I know, right? Sungyun chose her. She came by a few

days ago to inquire about the job opening." I notice a blue notebook on the counter, and without thinking much of it, I open it. The notebook is filled with dates and names.

> . . . (oral)/1987.3.24. Kim Sora (Donduk Female Merchant University. Sophomore. Tall-ish)/1987.4.1. Yeonsook Park (middle-school dropout. Fat. Bad body odor)/1987.7.25. Name unknown. (College student. Failed)

Sungyun snatches the notebook out of my hand. He is furious. What the hell was that? It looked secretive like North Korean spy codes. I think I saw Eunyong's name.

Today is turning out to be the worst. Sungyun constantly barks at me like an angry dog. *Wipe down the toilet seats. Why are these plates dirty? Who ate the fruit for sale? Smile at the customers, will ya?* It gets to the point that I throw down the rag and scream at him.

"Stop with all the nagging, Jesus Christ! Why are you so riled up? Fuck, you're acting shitty!"

"What? Shitty?! I know my aunt is spoiling you, but how dare you to keep calling me Sungyun. I'm way older than you, you know. Don't you notice everyone else calls me Oppa?" He goes on forever spewing this kind of nonsense. As he listens to his own case he seems to get angrier. He trembles, his fist curled tight. It looks like he's about to hit me. Eunyong pulls us apart, and the high school girl pretends not to watch us. *You fucker, you're some sort of pervert, aren't you? I know you invite women here after we close. Are you a serial cheater? A rapist?* What would happen if I started yelling

33

all this? What would he say? What would he do? You can't judge a book by its cover—I used to scoff at the saying, but I think in this case, it really might be true.

* * *

"Do you like working here? The owner said you're majoring in German Literature, right? How many years in are you?" the toothbrush salesman asks.

"I just finished my first year. I started working here a few months ago. I plan to quit soon though."

"Oh good! I need a German tutor. I was looking into getting a tutor or registering at the German learning institute."

That would be a great gig for me. Today has been shitty, but maybe things are looking up. The toothbrush salesman laughs loudly for some reason. He clarified earlier that he is a dentist, not a toothbrush salesman. He opened his office near Gupo, but there haven't been many patients. He thought it might be good for business if he had a few more certificates on the wall, so he is prepping for the German certification exam. He tells me he studied a little German in high school, so he'll be able to catch up quickly with my help, and playfully begs me to say yes to his proposal.

I don't really care about his back story. Tutoring is a good gig, much better than working at a café. And instead of tutoring some sniffling kids, I get to tutor a real man.

The shithead seems to be glaring at me—Sungyun, no, *segyoon*, a virus, a fungus. When I lift my head he makes a gun shape with his thumb and index finger. He pulls the trigger. He sends me the message through his body language: *You'll regret what you did. I will destroy you.*

I feel my belly grip with an ache. No one knows how much pain I'm in. There are many people who are actually sick inside even if they look alright. My uterus feels like it's been bombarded. It's my period. I wish I wasn't a woman . . .

Saved by the dog. The café owner stops by with Nana and immediately starts rambling about her fever. When I ask her if I may be dismissed early today, she lets me go without hesitation. *Person or animal, we all should take care of ourselves.* I thought about telling her I quit, but Sungyun, that virus in human form, butts in to talk to her about the grocery and alcohol delivery, so I decide I'll wait a few days.

Merry Gloomy Christmas

I fold up some toilet paper to squeeze into my panties. I have to walk slowly and awkwardly to keep the blood from leaking into my pants. I imagine that there is a philosopher slowly strolling through this city, brooding over deep philosophical thoughts, probably also constipated or on their period.

Jimin is probably also brooding over her deep thoughts or is on her period. When we started living together—well, ever since I started leeching off of her, to be specific—our period cycles started synching up. Together, we bleed profusely, struggling with the pain, and argue over the slightest provocations. We share sanitary pads and philosophy. Jimin doesn't know that she is the only member of humanity I love and emulate.

I wish there were more vacation days, red days, on the calendar. More of the admirable people on earth need to die off fast. People will like it; poor folks will be like, "Woo-hoo, another national holiday! Let's go for a picnic at the amusement park or in the tangerine groves!"

Christmas is not far off, so cloying Christmas carols fill the street. Variety stores are filling up with trees with twinkling lights and people picking out holiday cards. A child is laughing hysterically with a stuffed bear in her arms. Another child, probably her friend, presses the heart-shaped button attached to the bear's ear, and the hymn "You are Born to Be Loved" plays and gets stuck in my head. A red-eared child on a bike barely dodges a bus and pedals backward. I almost fall to the ground, shoved by the crowd. I had thought about buying a small poinsettia, but not anymore. I escape the main street to take a detour through a less crowded alley. The university's sound tech people are setting up a stereo system, so there must be a concert happening later. From the back of the half-finished stage, a man with a guitar calls out to a yellow-haired guy, yelling something about the amp and whatnot. There's a small sign that says DONATION-BASED CONCERT, but it's too dark for people to notice it. Even if, and that's a big if, Jimi Hendrix himself were to show up, people wouldn't notice. Nobody wants to hang out here.

I tell myself to stop thinking so negatively. But then another part of me barks back: Why do I need to change? Why do I have to choose between this or that? Is that the only option? I choose to run away from making a choice. Not to my father's place, nor my mother's place; like when my dad kicked me out and told me to find her, if she's even still alive. No, I'll go to both. No, there is nowhere to go. Joy to the world, whether the Lord is come or not . . . Look at me, I'm full of rambling anxious thoughts. I think this way because I'm anxious, and my anxiety makes me think this way. Why do I get more depressed as the day everyone else looks forward to so joyfully inches closer? I want to live a simple life. I don't care about finding myself or discovering my sense of identity. I just want to live anonymously. I grab my head and shake it. What's with me today? What is the origin of this endless anxiety? Don't think, don't think—but one thought tails another. This knot of unknowable angst can't be undone unless my intestines escape my body like it has been autopsied.

I walk along the serpentine, silent alley and come to the dead end. If I'd walked along at my normal pace, I'd already be inside Jimin's place by now. This is an unusually early time for me to be getting home. When I get home, she'll be so happy. If I tell her I'm going to quit my job at the café, she'll put her arms around my neck. Her hug will feel like choking, and I'll like that. Choke me tighter, I'll say. But my sneakers are leading me somewhere else, farther and farther away. They used to be white, but now they're dirty and gray, and they keep leading me somewhere other than where I'm trying to go. They lead me to avoid and evade where I should be going, like I'm a pack of rats led by a magic flute, or those red shoes that made the girl keep on dancing despite her broken ankles.

The alley is quiet. Darkness like a bottomless well. I don't see a light coming through the tiny record-sleeve-sized window of our place at the dead end of the alley. I guess Jimin isn't home yet. Where could she be? My legs hurt as I walk farther into the alley to get to our place. I rub my calves. I find myself not wanting to go inside the dark room alone. Should I just wait, squatting by the door, for Jimin? My body trembles, and my hands and feet are freezing.

When I open the door, it's dark. I feel a storm brewing in the darkness. My body trembles. In the dark, my left hand reaches for the familiar switch, but things get clearer in the darkness. Things I couldn't see at first in the darkness brighten and reveal themselves. I frantically wield my arms against the invisible storm, my arms and legs flapping like torn laundry hanging on the line. I fall into a well. No, I fly into it. I am aware of my place in the darkness, deep like a well. In the darkness, I'm the laundry that flies, a black plastic bag that flies. I'm the pills and powdered medicine spilled all over the floor, and I fly.

I'm the spilled glass, the pool of water, the white foam leaking out of her lips, and I float like vapor. I can't move. My body floated away, so I can't move. The crouching heap of something in the darkness screams. In the storming darkness, the sound of something being ripped apart—a wail, a shriek, a howl, none of the names fit—spills out.

"Jimin!"

I press the switch. The fluorescent light takes a few seconds to turn on, and those seconds are the darkest. Jimin is lying across the floor, as though she'd been thrashing in her sleep. Her long hair is tangled, but otherwise, she looks calm and composed. The spilled pills, the bottle, I leave everything as they are, and I lie next to her. The floor feels like cold dirt. I get up to get the blanket and shroud Jimin with it. I pull the other corner of the blanket over me. I reach out to hold her hand. It's cold, no longer soft. Her fingers are raw from her nail biting. I try to interlace my fingers with hers, but her fingers won't spread apart. Jimin's body is cold and hardened, like plastic. The noise of the workshop. The clanking lullaby of the machinery. I hold Jimin, as pretty as a doll, in my arms. I can't keep my eyes open, and I give in.

Part II

Death Mask

Another happy New Year: Happy 1988. Now there are two 8s, which looks like two nooses. Is this how it feels to stand on the gallows? The reality is that only the number on the calendar changes, nothing else. No . . . things did change.

My watch died but time kept moving, and everything fucking changed. My face was frozen and expressionless like a death mask as I packed, and, like a squeaky wheel, I tumbled into the attic room of Instant Paradise. Even after *that* happened, the sun continued rising and setting. The wind kept on blowing.

"Receive good fortune this year!"

I wish people wouldn't say shit like that. I hate imperatives. *I wish you a happy New Year* might be a little better. Happy, though? Me? This year? All this feels like a fucking joke. Even after I thought everything was over, here we are, another fucking year arrives. There's not much difference between yesterday and today, so why would one year or another be any different? What's so new about *this* year?

It's all bullshit.

I'm alive. I didn't freeze to death. I didn't starve to death.

Like my stepmom says, *I'm worse than vermin*, so here I am, still alive. Like she says, *I'm a cold bitch without a single drop of warm blood and without any tears*, so here I am, not shedding any tears. I stand by the window alone and awkward. From the window I watch the main street intersection leading to the university. A girl in a colorful hanbok dress holds her parents' hands, one of each, and swings between them. The sound of her laughter echoes up to my dark room. A mattress lies on the floor, the size of a coffin.

One Sunday, Sunbe and I were sitting on the windowsill at our place, sharing a bag of chips. *Should we move somewhere with a better view? To a higher floor? The rent will be higher though, huh? Let's just clean the place we already have.* Together, humming a song, we laundered our blankets by stepping on them in a tub full of soapsuds. She slipped and grabbed my arm. That day, we pulled the withering geranium from its pot and left the pot outside the door.

Another day, I thought Sunbe was calling me from the communal bathroom—maybe she forgot to take the toilet paper with her again. When I pushed open the door with a handful of toilet paper, Jimin was right outside, looking into the flowerpot we'd left there.

"What kind of plant is that? It looks like a little tree . . ." We looked at each other and smiled at this surprising new growth.

"You look stupid with your mouth hanging open like that. If you don't watch out, a fly will get in." Jimin tapped my chin and wrapped her arm around my shoulder. She spoke as though she was speaking to herself, rubbing my

44

disheveled hair. "If I wither and die like this geranium, you'll be a floating seed with nowhere to go. Go float somewhere nice and sprout, okay?"

"Why do you imagine me floating? Do you think I'm some sort of insect? A bee or butterfly or fly buzzing around?" I wrapped the toilet paper around my knuckles like a boxer and threw a punch at her. She giggled, swaying like a reed.

"I don't know when I might die, but when it happens, take all my books, okay?"

Did a white butterfly fly by at that moment? Did any of this even happen? The world is an impersonal space that keeps reminding us how small we are. When one organism disappears another takes its place. Everything just keeps on going, nothing matters.

Despite the calamity, no houses are collapsing. No hurricane flings people, struggling to hang on to the door, up into the sky. Not a single devastating epidemic circulates. The world doesn't come to a silent halt. I'm still breathing—in, out. I'm nothing but a breathing, grotesque death mask.

Alibi

"One ticket to Sanchung, please." This is the first time in the past few days I let a peep out of my mouth. I pull off my mitten with my teeth to count the coins.

"Same, please." As though she's been waiting for this moment the whole time, someone emerges from behind and nods as we make eye contact. It's Sol, my friend. "I was here the whole time, but you didn't seem to see anything. You look like a blind person. What are you going to Sanchung for?"

"Nothing, really."

"That isn't your hometown, is it?"

"Why are *you* going?"

"I'm trying . . . to go see . . . Jimin. It's been almost two months since she died, and I didn't make it to her 49th-day mourning."

"Yeah . . ."

"After stopping at Sanchung, I'm going to go home to Hadong. My mom's been sad that I wasn't coming home for Sul,[3] but the gas station I work at is busier during the holidays."

---

3. Sul is the Korean Lunar New Year.

46

"We can go together then. I'm going the same way."

Silence hangs between us. In any other situation, say, if we unexpectedly ran into each other on our way to the same concert, we'd be so ecstatic about the coincidence we'd jump up and down together. Well, we probably can't jump together. She has a bad leg, and she limps. Okay. We could've whistled a song together. On our way there, we might have bought a box of crackers, torn it open, and pasted them onto a messy sign to hold up at the concert. But instead . . . what is this distant chill that I feel? Her wistful gaze stabs at me like an ice pick.

I lean into the bus seat and close my eyes. The bus starts with a rattle. An announcement declares that it takes two hours and fifty minutes to get to Sanchung via Jinju. A soldier who looks younger than I do sits across the aisle from me. He takes his boots off and eats some gimbap rolls. The intense odor of his feet, his food, and the mildewy mopwater from the floor wafts up, making me nauseous. The driver blasts the heater and I'm suddenly claustrophobic. On top of that, the conversation between the couple behind me is unbearable. The man insists that now that an average Joe like Roh Tae-woo has become the president, the world is gonna get better. He calls the previous presidents, Kim Yong-sam and Kim Dae-jung, country-ruining bastards. His wife throws around words like *gukwisunyang* (nationalist pride) and gold medals, excitedly speaking of the '88 Olympics that will open in September. She speaks as though Roh Tae-woo single-handedly made the Olympics take place here this year. Don't they know Roh Tae-woo is not really that far off from the mass murderer, Chun Doo-hwan? I keep my eyes shut tight. I wish my ears had covers that opened and shut on command like my eyelids.

"Yeoul, are you asleep?"

"Yes."

"Very funny. Don't be like that. Listen to this song." Sol places her headphones over my ears. Kim Hyun-shik's song is playing from her CD player. "Isn't that nice?"

"Not really."

"He went to jail for smoking pot. The Wildflowers' Jeon Inguon and Huh Seongook were also arrested. There was a concert at the 63 Tower when they all got out ten days ago."

"Oh yeah? Did you have fun squealing like a stupid fangirl?"

"Well. I'm just trying to say . . . everybody goes through shit. People bounce back from it."

Sol seems to realize how empty and ill-fitting her words sound, and trails off. I feel like a lump of metal is hanging down my throat and sinking into my chest, lower and lower. I turn my attention to the song.

If I turn around and close my eyes, will I be able to forget? My beloved, what shall I do as you depart? I keep tripping over our memories of love. O these tears in both sets of eyes. I loved you. I didn't know then, but I loved you with my whole heart. Now I know. What love is, how much my heart hurts . . .

Now I know? Whatever. The heartfelt lyrics and husky voice don't resonate with me, it all sounds like noise.

I turn to Sol, "You and Jimin were in the same club, right?"

"I wasn't in the Blue Stockings, but I was a student representative with her in the Feminist Reading Group."

"I didn't know there was such a thing."

"Well, *that* happened not long after we started . . . why do you think she committed suicide?" Sol cautiously asks.

"I don't think she meant to go through with it. If she was determined to really end it, there should've been a note or something. Regardless, I don't think there is just one reason behind her decision."

"So what *are* those reasons? Shouldn't you know some of it? You lived with her."

"People keep telling me that, but . . . I feel like I knew so little of Jimin, perhaps even less than what everyone else saw in her . . . So even though it's too late, I'm trying to trace her path, get to know her . . ."

"At first, the student society considered connecting her suicide with the current regime's tyranny. Remember the Sunbe who threw himself off the library the night before the school festival? Last October?"

"Yeah, the one who tried to organize the Busan Gyungnam Student Association under the supervision of the National Student Assembly."

"The activist set himself on fire, screaming, 'Down with the military dictatorship.' He even left behind a letter written in blood with the slogan, 'Battle on.'"

"Yeah, now he's buried in the May 18th Memorial Cemetery. But I'm not following why you're bringing this up."

Sol continues: "Well, let me put it this way. During the Student Assembly meeting, some people in our student protest group voiced that we need to connect his suicide with her suicide. I know it's a stretch to connect a suicide for personal reasons with the rhetoric of student protest, even if she was an active member. Some voiced that doing something like that would make the whole student protest movement look bad. You know, and I heard Jimin had some sort of depression or dissociative disorder for a while. She had to take handfuls of pills every day, right?"

"Who the fuck is saying that?"

"Well, Hyangsook Unni . . . The pretty Sunbe with a cute mole on her nose? The one with the nasal voice? She said she was Jimin's best friend and knew everything about her."

"No, no, you've got it all wrong! Stop telling me this! Stop!"

"Don't get so upset, Yeoul! This is a secret, but . . . a few days before her death, Jimin asked me why pharmacies only sell sleeping pills one at a time, and if there were pills that could induce miscarriage. Why would she have asked that? She couldn't have been pregnant, could she? So today I plan to meet her parents and ask them why they cremated her body in such a hurry and why they didn't call the police . . ."

It's like Sol thinks of herself as some sort of detective, she almost seems excited as she rambles on. She got into pharmacy school as an honor student. She's booksmart, but she runs so goddamn slow. We met at a student protest and I had to drag her along. *Get up, do you wanna be trampled to death?* The riot police almost killed us both.

"Sol. Sol, Sol, shut up! People can hear you." People are stupid, like dumb beasts trying to sniff out the trail of another animal. They keep asking questions about her death as though that would lead them to know who Jimin was. In a way, I'm doing the same, I suppose. Perhaps the only thing a human can do without an ulterior motive is die.

I'm falling asleep again. Sleep roars in like a dark cloud. Someone told me I probably have narcolepsy and that I should get it checked out, but I savor these moments of drowsy ecstasy. I don't care if this is a disease. I would've died long ago if I didn't have this escape. The afternoon my mother left me, I slid down from the swing to curl up into sleep on the grass. When I heard about my stepbrother's death, I just keeled over and slept.

I see Jimin and me on the beach. We're making a sand castle, but the waves keep crashing in. Jimin chuckles. Our skin is bright pink. We look like a couple of baby piglets. She points at me and laughs. We're naked, but we don't feel embarrassed. The sun pricks our bare skin, it's the only thing we're concerned about. *Yeoul, I love summer. I wish I wasn't allergic to the sunlight.* Sunbe's back bloats up in bright red. *So itchy.* Her belly rises like a balloon. *Get in the shade before your belly bursts!* I try to yell but I'm merely mouthing the words. *Hurry! Hurry!* I mouth. But there isn't any shade, not even a tiny patch the size of a my hand. Ahead of us are vast sand dunes. I dig a hole in the shape of a mattress, and gesture to her to lie in it. She giggles, and lies down in the hole. All I need to do is cover her with sand. The sun can't get to her, and she can't keep inflating if I can cover her. I scoop the sand with my hands, but everything keeps slipping through my fingers. My hands are empty, and I panic. Sunbe's body is covered in red lesions, and, as she scratches, pus flows out. I poke my palm with my finger. My hand now has a hole in it. I poke my cheek with my finger. My finger penetrates my cheek until I feel the back of my head. I try to call to Jimin, I try to get back to her, but my feet are sinking in the sand.

Sol shakes me awake. "Yeoul! Are you alright? You were having a nightmare. Gosh! You're so sweaty."

"Where are we?"

"This is our stop. Can you get up?"

Pendulum

The bus terminal is full of people. The government desig-
nated Sul, the Lunar New Year, to be the "traditional" New
Year, and encouraged citizens to observe the first of January
instead, the "new" New Year. But people still travel in droves
to visit family on Sul. Today is the last day of the holiday, so
people are flocking to the terminal to return to work: sleepy
complaining children; *cough cough*—a young man who can't
stop his rattly cough; grandmothers and grandfathers seeing
off their children and their children's children; a middle-
aged lady with a bundled package on top of her head hand-
ing the load off to someone else; a chainsmoking old man;
a middle-aged man coughing and spitting up phlegm . . .
Sol and I leave the waiting room and walk toward the river.
The sky is gloomy and dark. It looks like it will pour at any
moment.

"The river where they scattered her ashes—that was
Gyungho River, right?"

"Yes, we were both there."

"Should we go to her parents' place and say hello? Do
you know where they live?"

"No! You can't do that."

"Why not?"

"Just don't."

"I want to ask them a few questions about her."

"Think about it. Do you really think they'd like it if we just barged in and started asking questions? Leave them alone."

"I can't decide if you overthink everything or just do everything on a whim. Let's go to the river then. We can cross the bridge over there, right?" She looks up. "It looks like it's about to rain, let's hurry."

Sol walks ahead of me, swinging a large bag in her hand as her black trenchcoat flutters around her body. Every time she steps on her left foot, her entire body slumps to the left as though the earth's axis were tilting. Walking behind her, I worry she'll fall on a patch of ice in the road and end up in tears.

★ ★ ★

I met Sol last May. We were singing "Marching Song for My Love" after watching the documentary about the May 18th Gwangju student protest that a few Sunbes had screened in the school theater.

"The burning oath we made: let's push on, leaving behind love, fame, and even names," we sang. The Sunbe with a microphone led the chanting, singing the phrase first, and the freshmen echoed him. We pumped our right hands, determined but restrained.

"Alright, you got the gist of the song, right? Which one of you wants to come onstage and sing it?" the Sunbe asked. Most freshmen shrank and looked away. The theater fell silent. Then a voice rang out, "Me! I'll sing." The voice came from right next to me. I turned and saw the face of a girl with a raised hand. She looked like a middle schooler. A young, innocent smile. Her wrists in the rolled sleeves of her yellow shirt were so thin, they looked as though they could snap right off. I watched the laborious process of her making her way to the stage: odd movements, like a bird trying her wings. She got up from her seat, walked down the stairs of the auditorium in her strange gait, and climbed the stairs of the stage, limping. The theater filled with swirling uncertainty. I couldn't quiet the rippling wave in my chest, so I escaped through the back door. The voice spilled out through the door, a delicate, bright, and yet solemn voice.

★ ★ ★

"Here."

Sol, like a fortune teller with a pendulum, stops at the corner of the river. She sets a newspaper down on a cold sand dune and anchors its four corners with rocks. "Ugh, this wind! Come on, help me out over here. Hold this down."

I notice a man standing on the bridge by his bicycle, watching us. My ears hurt so much they feel like they are going to fall off. Sleet, not quite rain or snow, scatters around us. I tilt my head back and catch the wet snow with my tongue; they are like icy flakes of a delicate wafer. The flakes land on the rushing water and become part of the river. I watch the river intently, standing like a crane. A crane doesn't watch the river because it's admiring the beauty of nature.

"The ashes floated away so we don't have to set things up right here." My voice is cold and detached.

"But don't you remember? This is the very spot you stood and scattered the ashes. I remember. We could see the pine forest ahead of us this way. We were away from the bridge, just like this."

"Everything looks the same around sand dunes like this. And with pine trees everywhere."

I don't want to do the ritual jul, the deep bowing. Sol insists on greeting Jimin this way, however. She lays down fruits, sponge cake, soju, and paper cups on the newspaper. After rummaging through her bag, she pulls out incense and a lighter.

"Do you see the jujube tree on the river bank over there? The single one among the zinnia trees. I can tell from that tree that this is the correct spot. My family used to run an orchard, so I know something about trees. They all look different individually, even when they are the same kind."

"Show-off."

"Why are you acting so sullen, like I dragged you here? You're too skeptical of every gesture." Nobody had ever told me I was too skeptical. I consider it a fault of mine that I trust others too much.

"You got it wrong. Sol, you're the one who's being outrageous. You prepared the whole Jesa ritual![4] I don't believe

_____

4. Jesa is a traditional ritual where one pays respect to the dead and other spirits, often with offerings of food and drink the dead person enjoyed in life.

in that kind of stuff, and I hate that kind of ritualistic crap. I just wanted to visit Sunbe's hometown and touch the river where Sunbe used to swim and fish."

"Yes. Also the place where we scattered her ashes. And you! You ate a handful of her ashes before we scattered them. I saw you sneaking it. Your lips got ashy. Do you think she'll live inside you forever now?"

Sol starts trembling as if she was freezing. Her lips are blue, and her hair, wet from the sleet, covers her tiny face. I take the jul, bowing deeply twice in the direction of the river. My teeth chatter. In the distance, I hear a loud crack, like the sound of a tree breaking. Sol mumbles, as if reciting a spell or a blessing.

"I'm gonna go now. What about you?" Sol asks me, frowning like she is about to freeze to death.

"I told you not to go to Sunbe's place!"

"Who said I'm going to her place? I'm going to *my* place. In Hadong. I'm going to stay with my parents during the break and move into the dorm at the end of the month."

As we pass by the riverbank, I turn to look behind me. Sol taps a dead-looking tree trunk. "This is a jujube tree. Even when the spring comes, it doesn't sprout. It too is skeptical of everything, so only after all the other trees have sprouted and blossomed will it slowly push out its new leaves."

"I can tell that you're insinuating something. Forget it. Just give me a light." After lighting the cigarette between my lips, I look at the watch on my wrist. It's the dead watch Jimin Sunbe gave me. My watch may be dead, but time keeps on going.

"Yeoul, can I ask you a favor? Please don't smoke at my place."

"What are you talking about? Who said I'm going to your place?"

"No, I mean, well . . . I'm just saying . . . let's go home together. You're so broke, you're practically homeless. Come to Hadong with me. Please?"

Sol leans in and tries to wrap her arm around my shoulder, but she's too short—shorter than an average middle schooler—so she hops. I lift my arm and pause, but eventually wrap it around Sol's shoulder. We walk askew, like they're the first steps we've ever taken.

A group of children run by, flying their kites. A man on a bicycle passes us, watching us through the corner of his eye. It's the same man who was watching us from the bridge. The red armband on his upper arm says *Watch Out for Wildfires*. I was told that Jimin Sunbe's parents farm in the area and during the winter work as wildfire watchers, which makes me think the man on the bicycle might be Jimin Sunbe's father. He and I exchange a look but don't say anything, just like at the funeral. His first daughter, the one who got married and moved to Seoul, hung herself; two years later, his youngest daughter was found dead in her apartment in Busan, so Korea must no longer feel like home. The pendulum of his heart circles and circles, never stopping in one spot. He spins the pedals of his bike and enters the dark forest. It doesn't seem like he'll ever reemerge.

Hitchhiker

Sol and I walk through a cold wind tunnel on a dusty street. No sidewalk. I'm so tired, I feel like flopping down on my butt and crying. Sol, silent through the entire journey, suddenly starts waving at a passing car. *Honk honk!* The passing car just honks at us. *Sol, what are you doing? Of course nobody would pick up hitchhikers in this remote area.* Sol, not discouraged, continues waving. It looks like she's dancing.

"Mom!" Sol hops and runs across the road, like a fish propelled out of a pond's depths to break free from the water. Making loud slapping noises with her shoes, she dashes over to a woman looking away from us on the opposite side of the road, and hugs her from behind. It looks so intimate. I wish I had someone I could hug from behind like that.

"Look who's here! I thought you were going to be here next week at the earliest." Her mom sounds more scolding than welcoming. She then turns to the car that has pulled up to the stand where she is selling apples. "No, I can't go any lower. No, not even a cent. I'm giving you such a good deal!" The car slowly pulls away and she yells after the car, "Okay okay. Just give me 4,500 won!" After the car leaves, Sol's mother clicks her tongue in annoyance. "City folk really don't give a damn about other people. Selling apples is a business with slim margins." Sol's mother shoves the money she just received into her fanny pack and starts to order Sol around as though her daughter never left for college and has always been at hand. Sol pulls out rotten pears from the boxes and collects them in the basket under the wooden platform. She then refills the empty rubber bucket her mother used with new apples.

"Mom, I brought a friend with me. We'll stay over for the next few days." Sol's mother doesn't respond to her announcement. Instead she asks if we had eaten. "Yeah, we ate a while ago. You know the grandma's seafood tent on the sidewalk next to the bus terminal? We ate the clam soup. We each had a whole bowl. It was so good."

"Yeah, hers is the real deal. All the other places dilute the soup, or use Chinese clams and lie that they are local Hadong clams." Even though I showed up unannounced on the evening of New Year's Day looking like a wet rat, soaked in sleet, Sol's mom offers me an apple after wiping it on her sleeve. I take a big bite of the shiny red apple. It's fragrant and sweet.

Selling fruit on the side of the road is not easy. We pile up the apples and pears, sitting on the wooden platform by the side of the highway. It's cold, so we blow on our hands and rub our red cheeks. A car stops. People mostly ask for the price, poke at the fruits, smell a few, but then leave. I feel an urge to walk into the road with a fruit basket in my hand. I could just lie down on the road and be done with it.

It's getting dark and no one is buying our wares, but still we wave at the cars with their headlights on.

"People must have eaten a lot of food and gotten full at

the New Year's rituals. Let's just go home." We walk past the green tea farm and reach the house on the hill. In its small yard, a dogwood tree is blooming, its flowers look like scattered yellow pills. Next to the tree, a pinwheel is spinning.

"Dad! I'm home!" Sol tosses her bag on the floor and yells at the top of her lungs. She throws open the doors.

"Your father went into town for an embalming. He won't be back till late."

"Again? Who died?"

"Now that the weather's warming up, there are funerals constantly. The night before the New Year, Hakgyu's uncle died, and then the town officer, who was healthy one day and then dropped dead the next." She gave a little *tut-tut* of disapproval. "Your dad had to go over to his place in the early morning."

"Tell Dad to get a new job. Choi at the morgue can take care of embalming, right? The village people keep calling me the embalmer's daughter. I don't like it."

"Don't be like that. When your father dies, this town will be full of ghosts who can't move on because your dad won't be there to embalm their corpses."

Sol's mother dozes off holding the spoon she was eating sikhye with. A grain of rice sticks to her lips. She must've been exhausted. Sol and I look at each other and quietly leave the room. We watch the river from the wooden deck. The dark river looks like teary black pupils. The moon drifts in and out of the clouds, reflecting on the water like an aluminum plate jaggedly cut with a serrated knife. *Why am I here? Where did I come from, and where am I going?* Such grandiose questions enter my mind. I thought I was just getting a headache from an infection in my wisdom teeth, but I feel worse. I think I have a fever. I could probably cook an egg on my forehead.

"It's too cold. Let's go inside." The bedroom Sol takes me into isn't heated, so it's freezing cold.

"Sol, feel my forehead." I grab Sol's hand and place her hand on my forehead to confirm my self-diagnosis.

"You're burning up! When did you notice this?"

"I dunno. I don't know why I'm getting sick! I wasn't *that* soaked from the rain."

"You haven't been sleeping well lately, though, right? You don't seem to eat right, either. When was the last time you took a shower? Frankly, you stink pretty bad. Your eyes are red, your cheeks are sunken . . . the bags under your eyes . . . it's as if you want to follow Jimin to the grave. You've changed so much, you suddenly seem old." Sol walks out of the room and leaves me standing there with her critique. She comes back with an electric blanket. Somebody must have been using it, because it already feels warm, like it's holding onto body heat. Sol turns the control dial to the maximum heat, and I lie down under the blanket, burying my face into the pillow.

"No, lie down the other way. Only dead people lie down with their head to the North." Sol pulls the pillow out from under me and slaps the back of my head. I sit up, spin on my butt to face the right way. Sol chatters away on her belly, resting her head on her hands. Her shirt is loose, so the neckline hangs enough to show her clavicle and pale breasts. I feel lightheaded and dizzy, but she won't stop telling me stories about her life: how her father and grandfather cheered *hurrah* at the sound of her first cry at birth—how her cry was so loud they thought she was a boy—how she excelled in school—both in her studies and on the track team. I think about her limping gait as we ran together at the student protest but say nothing. She tells me how she once hid in her closet and didn't come out for days. I feel thirsty and worn out from fever. I wish she would stop talking so we can go to sleep. Sol doesn't seem tired at all. Like a kid on an overnight field trip, she talks on and on even with the lights off. She doesn't realize my mind is scrambled like a shaken up bento box. She goes on about a time eight or nine years ago: black fungus was going around the orchards, and the disease turned all the pears black, starting at the stem. The helpless villagers could only sigh in response. Sol's family's orchard was hit especially hard, so the local journalists did a feature story on them. It was on that fateful day that it happened: it was cherry blossom season and tourists were coming in droves on buses. Sol was playing jacks alone in the shade behind the tour buses, and a bus backed up onto her. Sol tells me she was lucky, she could've been squashed into roadkill, but she only got a limp from the accident.

I'm pretending to be asleep, pretending I'm not listening. In the darkness I open my eyes to steal a glance at her face.

How long did she suffer before she got to the point where she can talk about this like it was an ordinary thing, without tears, without pain? How long did she hide in the closet, watching herself crumple in disbelief?

My pillow gets wet, and the fever seems to break. I want to reach out and hug my friend, but I don't want her to know I've been listening after all. Or am I afraid I won't be able to release her once I hug her? I stop myself from reaching out and instead wrap my arms around myself.

I don't know how long I've been asleep—I feel a rush of hot air. Not long ago all I felt were the claws of the cold draft seeping under the door and in through my blanket, skinning me alive. Is the heat inside of me burning up this room? What is this smell? Is someone blowing heated hot breath on me?

"Fire! Fire! Wake up!" Sol yells. The blanket is ablaze. Flames flicker like the tongue of a ghost on the edge of the blanket I had been pushing down with my heel. Sol and I together grab a pillow and blanket and use them to smother the flame. The fire goes out too easily and in our shocked state it seems like a joke. It must have been an electrical fire. The electric blanket is blackened on the edge.

"We survived!" We playfully slap each other and giggle.

Wedding Cake

Will you marry me?

A Post-It's hanging on the door. A basket of roses at the doorstep. I scoff. Probably the lover of someone who used to live here must've sent this, or some idiot who doesn't even know where his lover lives. I push the rose basket away with my foot. I click my teeth as I push the key into the door-knob, and just then the door opposite mine opens. A man with bird-nest hair briefly emerges but then slams the door, startled at the sight of me.

I don't know what kind of people live here. I think four or five people live on this floor. There are ten or so pairs of shoes that step on each other and are being stepped on in the foyer. Sungyun's room is right before the foyer.

Nana's mom, the café owner, told me to go out and take down the sign that says ROOM AVAILABLE OVERNIGHT. She goes on, "Eunyong told me about your situation—she was freaking out the whole time. Are you planning on going back to your old place? I don't think you can stand your place anymore. Just try to forget everything. You can stay here. We have a room you can use. You can trust me. Don't worry about the rent." She quickly added, "In return you

can come to the café early, help with the cleaning and grocery shopping with Sungyun."

That was a month ago. I climbed these stairs with Sungyun
making snide remarks at me. It was the same day the
scary-looking men in red cotton gloves arrived at Jimin's
place with the moving truck. They took everything: books,
clothes, right down to the last spoon. That was when
I returned from Jimin's funeral, I'd spent the day lying cata-
tonic in the corner of the room like unwanted rebar in a
junkyard.

I fall stiffly on top of the mattress. The woman who
lived here before me left behind a few things, including
several bloodstains on the mattress—from what, a nose-
bleed? Her period? Something else?—and a red cord. The
cord is for hanging laundry and spans the distance between
the walls.

I'd hung my towels, socks, and underwear after washing them, but two pairs of underwear are missing now. Did
someone come in while I was away? But then I never know
where my mind is. I can't trust myself. The gloves I'd been
wearing when I left home are gone now too. I might have
left them by the river, or in the bus, or at Sol's place. I have
no recollection of what's been happening, as if some device
has been jammed into my head to prevent me remembering.
Everything feels like it happened last night or eons ago. At
this rate, after washing my face one day, I may ask my reflec-
tion, "Who are you?" If that day comes . . . well, that doesn't
sound too bad.

My room is cold. I think it's colder *in* the room than

66

outside. Where're my cigarettes? Oh right, Sol confiscated them. She's probably getting yelled at by her parents. *We let her stay over, and she took off without even saying goodbye? She has no manners! She brought bad luck to us. Why else would the electric blanket catch fire?* I feel like I can hear it. I throw the blanket over my head and plug my ears, but I cannot sleep. *Please, please, please. Gurgle.* I hate these hunger-bugs in my stomach, I can't help them. I guess I'll make some ramen.

★ ★ ★

"Yeoul, when did you get here?" The café owner is so happy to see me that she claps at the sight of me. The café was closed during the holidays, and today it reopened. Even so, why is she here so early? She starts chattering, telling me all the things I didn't ask about. *I went to your apartment with New Year's rice-cake soup, and you weren't there. Where were you?* She dances like a girl trying out her favorite pink shoes. She spins. "What do you think? I'm wearing this for the wedding rehearsal." The purple dress she is wearing has a plunging neckline and is trimmed with fur from shoulders to chest.

"It's too form-fitting for my taste . . . But, Ajumma,[5] you'll wear it if you like it, so . . ."

"It's a fault of yours that you can't lie. This is an expensive dress! Can't you just say it's beautiful? And *Ajumma*? Don't call me Ajumma. I told you to call me Unni! Okay. Let's try it again. Call me Unni!"

---

5. *Ajumma* is used to address an older woman.

Jumping out of nowhere Sungyun suddenly chimes in. "You'll see. She'll never call you that. She calls everyone by the terms that *she* wants to use. She calls me Sungyun-si,[6] like I'm a stranger or we're same age. If she doesn't feel like it, she won't even talk to me for days!"

What the hell? Today Sungyun is wearing a shiny black suit, a floral tie, and even a handkerchief. It looks good on him. This is the first time I've seen him in anything other than sweatpants and a T-shirt.

"Okay, let's establish the terms we address each other with," the café owner says. "Call Sungyun *Oppa* and call me *Unni* from now on. Doesn't that sound nicer? 'Unni,' it feels warm, intimate. People at the wedding would be surprised if they heard you calling me Ajumma! That'd sound rude and distant!"

"I'll call you Sajang-nim,[7] then," I say.

"You are so stubborn! Whatever. I won't stand for it if you call me Sajang-nim or Ajumma ever again. And let's buy you some new clothes! Even Sungyun looks so handsome now that I dressed him up. He looks like a nobleman."

The café owner seems to find me beneath her. Ever since I moved into her building, she treats me like her dog, Nana. Eat this. Wear that. She once offered me a cookie that she had taken a bite out of and offered me her old leather jacket and her see-through blouse. They didn't fit me, and I didn't like how they made me feel, so I placed them in

6. *Si* is an honorific added to a name to make the address formal, used when speaking to a person of equal social standing who is not a family member or close friend.

7. *Sajang-nim* is used to address one's boss in the workplace.

the café's kitchen cabinet, and later I saw Eunyong wearing them—she seems to enjoy them. Now the café owner's trying to force me into calling her Unni . . .

I speak with my own mouth, so I will address others on my own terms. Other girls called Jimin Unni, but I called her Sunbe. I didn't have a particular reason for it. I just liked it that way. My stepmother tried to coax me into calling her *Mom*. She said in return, she'd give me back the special pillow that smelled like my mother. My ragged but precious pillow, which she kept on top of the armoire, just out of my reach. I didn't want to call her *Mom*. I addressed her by "Excuse me" or "Umm," and she'd slap me across the face. I can't count how many times that happened. Without the pillow I had a hard time falling asleep, and even if I fell asleep, I got sleep paralysis. When my family slept over at my older uncle's place for the Jesa ritual, I had to bring the pillow with me in a large paper bag. With incredible cruelty my stepmother made me watch her burn the pillow. What an awful human being. But I'm not trying to paint her as the fairy-tale stepmother-witch here. Not all biological mothers make warm bowls of white rice and wait for their children to come home like textbooks will have us believe, either.

* * *

"Yeoul! Yeoul! Where is she hiding again?"

Seething with anger, I'm trying to eat a bowl of rice soaked in cold water in my room, but the café owner bothers me before I can even eat the second spoonful.

"Yeoul, check on the cake we ordered at the bakery. See if they are making it tri-layered like I asked. I told them it should be topped with a white chocolate angel. I thought the rose decoration they had on the sample cake was tacky. Check that they've done that, and also double-check with them on the delivery time. Remind them I want the cake on Sunday, and that the traffic to Haewoondae gets really bad on the weekend."

Reluctantly, as slowly as possible, I go downstairs to the bakery, pushing the door open with my shoulder. The year I got accepted to the university, this had been a bookstore. I used to browse books here. The owner, a young man with Coke-bottle glasses, helped me find Michael Jackson posters and recommended social science books published by small presses like Mung Bean Press, Raven Press, and Rock Pillow Press. He said I didn't even have to buy books to hang out here, I could just read them there as long as I didn't wrinkle the pages. This was the place where I bought the *Dictionary of Aesthetics Theory Terms* for the Aesthetics Theory class I took. (I ended up not really reading the book. I don't really know what I was doing signing up for that class.) But one day, the New Day Bookstore became the New York Bakery. As with most of the buildings near the university, this building is now filled only with stores for entertainment and food. Oh wait, the fourth floor is for lodging, so my observation isn't entirely true. The first floor became a bakery, the second floor a café, and the third floor a billiard parlor. The café's sign—INSTANT PARADISE—is the biggest. At night the sign flashes garishly in the dark. The building owner's store sign dwarves those of the renters. Faced with this unfair reality, are we just supposed to shrug and say, *That's just the way things are?*

Matryoshka

"Do you think he married her for her money?" I ask the toothbrush salesman—I mean, the dentist who's now become a regular at the café.

"What?" he asks.

"You told me he's four years younger than the café owner, right? He's a handsome bachelor. Ajumma has married two or three times now. So . . ."

"I think they married because they love each other. No one outside a relationship can know what goes on between a couple."

"Even if that's the case . . . It hasn't been very long since you brought him here and introduced them to each other. Don't you agree?"

He sits at an angle and looks straight into my eyes. His irises seem small in relation to the whites of his eyes. His facial expression is that of a crane waiting for the right moment to snatch up a fish from the river, focusing. I suddenly feel embarrassed and annoyed. Like the fish head Nana likes to chew on, my head droops. With the sudden silence in the conversation, the music in the background grows louder.

"You must like Leonard Cohen. I noticed that you put on his album," he notes.

I got the vinyl record that's playing now in the café as a gift from this person sitting across from me.

It was the night of the café owner's wedding. Out of the blue, he gave me the record. The café was closed that day, and everyone had gone to the wedding hall at the hotel, and I was left alone with Nana at the café. I was reading about Italian baristas because I'd started to appreciate coffee. Several times I'd asked the café owner to buy an espresso machine so we could make espressos and cappuccinos, but she said the machine was too expensive. She wasn't even replacing the worn needle on the record player, so we couldn't even play music in here—she kept saying tomorrow, tomorrow . . . the uncultured bitch.

I felt tired without music. Spacey. I found myself mind-lessly chewing my nails, and that made me angry. I was lying on the sofa, throwing peanuts into the air and trying to catch them in my mouth. The peanuts I missed scattered across the floor. Nana was asleep on my belly. The café owner said she'd be in Guam or Saipan or wherever for seven days for her honeymoon, so I thought that as long as I could hide from Sungyun's watchful eyes I could be lazy and pick on Nana. But since the early evening Nana had been depressed, not being her usual playful self, and kept on sleeping. The dentist opened the door, entered the café, and stumbled toward me. He said he didn't feel good about his best friend marrying the café owner and mumbled something about how he regretted introducing him to her. He had hoped to live with his friend in the house the friend had designed, but that was all moot now. I liked him better now that he was drunk. Until then we had been using the honorific tone with each other—awkward and uncomfortable. It was nice to finally speak casually. He walked into the DJ booth and removed the old needle with his trembling hand. He pulled out a new needle from his pocket, and in a familiar movement placed the new needle in the arm. He placed a record on the turntable, and the needle nimbly moved along the grooves of the record.

Fortuitously, the fourth track, the same song he played that night, is playing in the café right now: "I'm Your Man."

> If you want a boxer
> I will step into the ring for you
> And if you want a doctor
> I'll examine every inch of you
> If you want a driver, climb inside
> Or if you want to take me for a ride
> You know you can
> I'm your man.

I think the song is saying, "I'm here for you." The man sings in a slow, cloying voice, viscous like honey. I cringe, but I don't hate his voice. I close my eyes. What if I could find a "doctor" like in the song who would "examine every inch of me?" I anticipate the dentist rising from his seat. He is going to. He has to. He is going to approach me, sit next to me, and touch me. He will kiss my forehead, my nose, and continue descending . . . I wet my lips with my tongue. I've never kissed a man before. If I'd known an opportunity like this would arise, I would've brushed my teeth. I had raw onions with black noodles for lunch. I close my eyes and my eyelids tremble. *What is taking so long? Should I open my eyes? Won't you kiss me? I don't need you to kneel and beg for my love like in the song. Don't you like me? No, you're just a coward. I can't wait. I won't wait. I will show you how this works. I'll undo my buttons one by one. I will caress your cheek, kiss you, then you will hold my hand.*

"Hey! Yeoul! What are you doing, praying? Didn't you hear me come in? Were you asleep sitting upright like that? There are customers here!" When I open my eyes, everything is blurry and slowly clears up. Shit, how embarrassing. Eunyong makes a spinning motion with her index fingers by her temple. The dentist and Sungyun are looking at me with confused looks on their faces.

Gwak Eunyong, do I seem crazy to you? Why did you get back so soon anyway? You told me you were going to play billiards in the parlor upstairs with Sungyun. Can I even call you my friend when you choose the worst time to return and ruin things? I hold back all these accusations that want to spring out of my throat, and I gulp down a glass of water. I can't get a read on the dentist. Does he have any emotions or desires, or is he like the dentures and toothbrushes in his pocket, inanimate and emotionless? Or maybe he's like a matryoshka, a Russian nesting doll? There might be a different face beneath the face I see, and then yet another.

Proxima Centauri

We are closing the café early tonight. As if they could sense the absence of the owner, customers are not coming today. We choose not to be industrious workers. I feel zero guilt— like the time I peed in the communal bath. Sungyun followed the dentist to try out his new car. There's nobody to bother me and Eunyong. It feels like the café is under siege. Is this what Jimin was talking about when she talked about seizing the means of production? Would she give me a noogie for simplifying her ideas if she knew I was making this connection?

I take a beer from the fridge. It's an imported kind that I've never had before. Eunyong slices a pineapple for snacks. "Bring some bananas and cheese too!"

We raise our glasses for a toast. We can replace the café's food we're eating, and I have some spare money.

I've been tutoring the dentist in German, but the further we progress on the lessons, the less sure I become about the lessons I am "teaching." Whenever I get stuck, the dentist quickly looks up the word in the dictionary. Eunyong ostentatiously walks by our table to mutter, "Who's tutoring who?" That bitch. Her knowledge of English only extends to greetings like *Hello, oh my God, sorry,* and she doesn't know a word of German, not even the alphabet.

What matters is that I got some money from tutoring my older student. A small part of me feels guilty—he gave me twenty thousand won in advance, and we've only met twice for the lessons. But then he gave me another envelope of money. I've decided I'm going to study German hard myself and teach him well this month. There isn't any part-time gig as easy as this one. I don't want him to look for a tutor who is actually competent. If I save this tutoring money for the next three months, I can cover my university tuition. Then I could proudly announce my official emancipation from my dad and declare why I left home.

"Eunyong! Bring more beer! I can't even get up right now."

"You sound so drunk. I saw you throw up earlier. We gotta stop drinking. We've been drinking all these . . . shit. How much is this gonna cost us?"

"It's fine, it's fine . . . Just bring more, okay!" As I yell, my voice rings in my ears. It sounds unfamiliar, foreign—like someone else's voice. Like when you record your voice on a blank cassette tape and play it back.

I used to record my favorite pop songs on empty cassettes, singing into the tape to hear my own singing. I thought I lost those tapes, but then I discovered that my stepbrother had been listening to them. He used to peek in to watch me bathe too. Crazy asshole.

•

Why does everyone I love leave me? Why do they abandon me or drop dead? Tears start flowing uncontrollably. Fuck it, I wanna die too. I chew on my agony. Well, no, actually, what I'm chewing on is this cheese.

"Ugh, the worst thing a drunk woman can do is cry. My mom used to cry after a few glasses of soju too. Jesus. Didn't know you were the type who cries. Here, drink this and sober up." Eunyong hands me a glass of ice water. I gulp it down to choke down my wail. "How do you feel? Yeoul, you are skinnier than me, taller than me, and you get to go to college. If you cry and pity yourself, that's just bullshit. Stop it! You're a spoiled little bitch if you don't stop crying."

"That's true."

Eunyong curses, lies, and plays hooky fluently. She doesn't seem like that on the surface. A lovely girl. But I won't love anyone ever again. The people I love died because of my love—I know they are with me at all times, hovering around me. How many things are right next to me but can't be seen? Like Proxima Centauri, the dark star nearest to Earth, this strange planet I stand on, but can't be seen. Ghosts. Protective spirits. Devils. Devils with angels' faces. All these confusing things. The invisible hands that constrict my throat. *What the fuck are you rambling about?* The couch shouts from the corner. The ashtray tries to get my attention. *My darling, you were wonderful tonight*, Eric Clapton on the wall winks at me. I sense that someone is waiting for me behind the wall.

"I miss you," I mutter.

"Who are you talking to?" Eunyong grabs my shoulder and shakes impatiently.

"None of your business. You have no idea. You don't have to know everything."

"I know what's going on. You like him, don't you?"

"Who?"

"Who? Of course I mean the dentist."

"Haha, whatever. Imagine away! I gotta lie down." I hit my head on the table, and rub my cheek.

"He seems to like you too. I am good at reading men. He has money and he seems nice. So get him! Sink your claws in."

"Get him? Am I a cat and him a mouse or something?"

"Okay. Hear me out. I got the art of seduction down. I'm gonna teach you a thing or two. Hey! Don't fall asleep. Wake up, Yeoul. Shit. We drank too much. We need to replace what we drank. Where's the money, Yeoul? I'll go to the supermarket."

"It's in the kitchen drawer."

Eunyong rolls on her side on the floor to get to the kitchen. I hear the *clink-clank* sound of her going through the drawer and see her emerge with the envelope of money and a picture. It's the picture of Jimin and me. We took a picture in front of the flower tree in the university garden. We are holding hands, smiling awkwardly.

"I swear I've seen her before." Eunyong scratches her crotch, sniffs her fingers, and tilts her head.

"No way. Don't touch that picture with your dirty hands." I try to get up to take the picture away from her and almost fall over.

"Hold on a sec." She holds the picture away from me, just out of reach. "I'm good with faces. I remember every single person who's ever walked into this café. I've impressed several customers with that skill, you know. I've definitely seen her before. Not at the café though . . . Yeah! I remember now. I was on my way to the café, and I saw her screaming at Sungyun at the top of her lungs in the back alley. He kicked her down and I intervened. Who is this woman? Why are you so protective of this photo? She isn't the one who killed herself, is she?"

Face-Off

Lately, Sungyun is MIA, not even his shadow can be found. It's been a week, and I've been searching for him. The café, the alleys, the billiard parlor. I knocked on the door of his place several times a day, but not even a peep. Neither Eunyong nor the café's owner has seen him recently. I don't think Eunyong would've warned him that I am looking for him like a bloodhound. The more he avoids me, the more my suspicion that he has something to do with Jimin's death grows. Eunyong said she saw them fighting in the back alley after the presidential election. She said it was around the time the Christmas carols started playing in the streets, when the bakery had a promotion on their cheapest cakes. Jimin died around then. Sungyun didn't tell me that Jimin visited the café to see me, nor that he offered her a drink when she was getting up to leave. While I was wasting away with sadness, Eunyong and the café owner had harassed me with the questions about Jimin—about her appearance, personality, suspected reasons behind her suicide, her family history—but Sungyun, unlike his usual nosy self, stayed out of it. I can't focus on anything—my hair is bristling—until I track him down with my sharp nose. I can't stop until I grab him and break his neck.

The street has regained its vitality now that school is in session. I walk past the seasonally exotic decor of a new café, past a group of college students looking at all the vendor carts with their various accessories, and arrive at a scrap metal shop in the back of a building. I ask for a crowbar, but the old man with a skewed spine gives me a hammer that looks like an ax, which he calls a *biru*. It's expensive, but I buy it without hesitation. I pay five hundred won for some metal wire, too. As I leave, I get paranoid that a man with hair gelled and propped up like a rooster's comb is following me, so I enter the arcade and hide in there for a while.

I go into the café kitchen and get a knife. I walk up to the fourth floor, and the stairs rattle under my feet as though they are actually made of rotting wooden planks. My footsteps—*thump, thump*—ring loudly. The decal on the window of the billiard parlor, with crossed cues that look like a giant forbidding X, warns me not to proceed. But I continue up the stairs. I'm just trying to open a door, that's all. I feel it, the compulsion, precognition, even a sense that all this is destined to be. I know I have the right to unlock this door. The right? Am I thinking about ethics right now? Is this act an ethically justified act? Why am I worrying about justice? The image of Raskolnikov killing the hag appears in my vision. This is what I get for my bad taste in books. The so-called Western canon only encourages my paranoia.

I open the door to the vestibule. Another door presents itself. My hand holding the knife trembles. The skin on the back of my hand looks rough, and the veins are popping out—it looks like a hag's hand. It's so quiet. I bend the wire and push it into the keyhole, barely larger than a needle's eye. It doesn't open, even as I struggle to poke and jiggle the doorknob. I push in the knife at the gap between the door and the threshold and twist it. The knife blade comes out gnarled. I don't know what to do with my *biru*. Why can't I make this hole do what I want? I stab the hole again and again. *Open, open, goddamn it!* Cold sweat bubbles up on my skin and trickles down. At any moment Sungyun could leap out of nowhere and grab my neck, yet the door refuses to open.

I turn around and sit down, trying to take my shoes off. I'm angry when I catch myself adhering to indoor etiquette out of habit, even in this kind of situation. I put my shoes back on, tighten my laces, and start kicking the door. The door rattles. Alright. I'll kick harder. I'll kick until the door breaks open. I don't care if I break my leg. I take a few steps back to ram my shoulder against the door. Again. The door of someone else's room opens, and a woman looks out to see what's going on. Another door opens, and a man notices the knife, wire, and wood chips from the door on the floor. I shake the *biru* in my hand and make a face at them to go back in. We all live in the same flat, but we don't know each other at all. Just as they shoot back into their rooms, Sungyun's door unexpectedly opens.

"Get in!" He grabs me and pulls me into the room, locking the door.

"Why didn't you open the door if you were home? How long have you been here?"

Sungyun covers my mouth with his hand and quietly whispers. "Are you going to be quiet? Or do you want to fucking die?"

I blink. *Yes, I'll be quiet,* and he pushes me onto the bed. The blanket is creepily white and soft. The room is freshly done with pearly white wallpaper. It looks like a brand-new room. The room is several times larger than mine. It's nearly unbelievable that such a nice room exists in the same building I live in. The shower is made of curved glass, and a window with white blinds halfway open looks out over the city. Sungyun opens the refrigerator next to the washing machine and grabs a beer from it. He looks too calm, almost as if he had been expecting a guest. The place looks freshly tidied, and he looks like he just finished taking a shower.

"Do you want some beer?"

I bend up my knees to my chest, wrap my arms around them, and hold myself. "What did you do to Jimin?"

"Why are you in such a hurry to learn everything? Don't worry. I'll tell you. Drink up while it's cool." He pours the beer into the glass; the foam rapidly rises like it'll go over the lips of the glass but stops short, and the head sits perfectly.

Along the wall there is a wooden display case filled with various objects: a bronze doll playing violin, a colorful elephant sculpture, and multiple picture frames. One of the frames has a naked woman in it. She is wearing a pair of dark sunglasses, so I'm unsure, but it looks like Eunyong. I realize there are about ten pictures of nude women—one curled up into a ball with her cleavage showing between her knees, another woman with disheveled hair with her hips high in the air. None of them look like models or porn stars. *What the fuck?* Manet's *Olympia* innocently lying on her side, Gustav Courbet's *L'Origine du monde*—her pink areola, her milk-colored belly button, her thick, black, mossy pubic hair—I could draw them with my eyes closed. I kept prints of the paintings in my desk drawer during high school. They're unmistakable. Why did he put my favorite paintings alongside these photographs?

"I know you. I can pick out your scent even when you are several feet away from me. I knew we'd click the moment I saw you. It took longer than I thought, but today is the day. You want me, don't you?"

I try to throw the beer he gave me at him. He grabs my wrist, and the glass merely falls over. He isn't even alarmed at my outburst.

"Is that how it's gonna be? Come on, I was being nice. With the expensive stuff I put in your drink, you should be feeling pretty good by now, no? You stupid bitch." He slaps my face, tears the shirt off my chest, and bites into my breast.

"You fucking filthy animal! You filthy shit!" Trying to get away from him, I arch my back like a bow. I kick his head, my feet still in the sneakers.

"You bitch, it's only gonna get more fun." The asshole hits my face with his fist. Once. Twice. Three times. Again. Again. Blood from my nose sprays across the room. My lips feel ragged and torn. It doesn't hurt, however. The fucker pushes his mouth onto mine, and quickly pulls down my jeans. His mouth travels down, stops at the pubic mound covered in underwear, and blows his warm breath onto it.

"Help! Is anyone there? Help!" I scream.

He reaches under the bed, pulls out a long scarf, and folds it neatly. He pushes it between my lips and ties a knot at the back of my head. He pulls out a rope and ties my arms behind me. He seems familiar with the process. He sniffs deeply into my underwear that somehow he has taken off of me. *Sniff, sniff.*

"Well then, it's picture time." He claps three times and walks away, cheerfully swinging his hands, and returns with a camera. It's the same kind of Polaroid camera that I asked my father to get for my birthday.

Dad. It's all your fault that this is happening. You wanted me dead, didn't you? Why did you trust my stepmother but not me? Did you even look at me, see me as I was? Why did you abandon Mom and me? If you abandoned me, why did you take me to that den of danger? What did I ever do to you? It's not my fault that Hyunwoo died, you know that right? I did my best. That's just me. I miss you. I miss you, Mother. Give me wisdom, give me strength. Take me away before I break even further. Mother!

I writhe and cry. I will not cry "mother" out loud, though. I know from experience it's no use to cry for mother. And it's difficult to cry because of the gag in my mouth. Get it together, Yeoul! Was my impulse to attack Sungyun really a misunderstanding of my deeper desire to run away? I felt like I had to do something, as a revenge for my whole life where bad things keep on piling on top of each other. I stop writhing and struggling and lie there on my side. The asshole is looking at the freshly printed pictures he has taken. He looks satisfied, standing tall like a large, filthy statue.

Okay, you're gonna take pictures? Fine! Out of spite, I open my legs wide. Wider than the woman in *L'Origine du monde*. My labia must be fully parted, and the pink bits must be sticking out. My arms hurt behind me, but I smile with my eyes. I bring my knees together and draw them to my forehead. *Do you like this pose? Does this make you hard, you fucking asshole?* I can't believe that my knowledge of nude paintings has led to this moment.

"Hmm. Good, keep going."

I hear the sound of his Polaroid printing. But the machine in my head isn't turning. What should I do next? Should I pose like the woman in *Le Déjeuner sur l'herbe?* I think my head is bleeding. Should I lie on my side like Olympia—cross my legs and look defeated? Will a black maid bring me flowers like in the painting?

The monster licks my asshole. With complete disregard for what I want, the dog licks with his nimble and wet tongue, like Nana licking her bowl. My eyes close. I feel like shitting.

"Nngh! Nngh!" I shake my head, and make a gesture asking to untie me. *You fucking bastard. You fucking monster. You fucker, even the word* fuck *is too good for you. Answer my question. Is this what you did to Jimin? You raped her, didn't you? Did you impregnate her? Fuck!* I feel my eyes bulge out of my skull, and I dry heave.

The monster pulls down his zipper and takes his pants off. He pulls at the waistband of his boxers to check on his penis, shrugs, and walks toward the shower. This is my chance. I get up, and run to the door. I bang on the door with my head. Please, please, open! The monster grabs my leg. He grabs my hair and pulls hard. The naked monster laughs, dripping with water. Suddenly, there is the sound of the lock being unlocked. The monster tries to stop the door from opening, but he is too late.

"Oppa, it's alright, it's just me. Are you hungry? I brought some fried chicken . . ." Eunyong enters with a bag of fried chicken in her hand. I shoot through the door. The door is wide open. I stumble toward the stairs. The monster must have kicked me in the back—the next thing I know, I'm tumbling down the stairs. I imagine my naked body folding, crumpling into a ball, rolling somewhere far far away. My flesh crumbles into tiny flakes. I'm glad that I can't see myself—there is no anger, no resentment, only darkness. I hear someone calling for me. The darkness is deep as a well, so dark, how did my mom get here? How did Mom and Jimin come find me in this cold storm, in bare feet no less? They are waving and calling my name. Why are they laughing?

Part III

Formaldehyde

Heheh. The sound of someone laughing wakes me up. I find the corners of my mouth pulled wide—it was me who was laughing. Yes, right, I was once a child who laughed easily. My head feels clear. *It's time to get up.* My body flinches but remains lying down. *Lazy ass.* I take the lazy ass's side in this decision-making and stay lying down. Huh, I'm wearing clothes, unfamiliar blue cotton clothes . . . both sides are open, held together by strings carelessly tied to cover my privates . . . barely. I look at my surroundings. There are close walls all around me. Is it raining outside? I hear low snoring sounds. Where am I?

I think someone is on a low cot next to me, but I can't tell who it is from where I am. My left arm is in a cast, and the ends of my fingers stick out from the top. I try moving the fingers. All this is real. I'm not dreaming. I lift my right hand up to touch my head to see if it's caved-in. No, it's still round. I feel several bandages though. The light in the ceiling is dim. I'm glad of that. How about my legs? My left leg seems fine. My right leg is in a cast and is elevated. Even though all this seems to suggest I'm in serious condition, I feel indifferent. Everything probably turned out the way it ought to. I could've shattered, like an iconoclast against a sculpture of an idol, completely and irreparably. But here I am, I survived to continue being an inconvenience. I feel like King Kong at the arcade—I have to keep on fighting in order to eat the banana worth 500 points. I need to keep on fighting to level up and save the princess. Am I also programmed by someone to keep on going?

I don't know. If only I could say, *I didn't mean things to turn out this way, none of this was intentional, there was no other way, so goodbye,* and then die. That'd be all.

I can tell I'm at a hospital. I can tell by the smell. As I think this, I hear it in the monster's voice. Is it that monster on the other cot? I consider using my *biru* to smash him to smithereens. I feel like it's unfair to take my revenge while he is asleep, but still I want to smash his skull. What's stopping me is not my ethics but my immovable body. Heh, I guess I'll postpone things yet again. I haven't even figured out my life, how dare I take another's? Does anyone know the meaning of life? Does a fish know the meaning of water? Does an apple tree know the meaning of the sun? Did the monster get a taste of Monster World and come to understand it? Does the monster know what to do next? Why does my mind waver so much? With my body in this mess, my mind must've weakened. Why else would I be imagining the monster's point of view? Am I feeling more sympathetic toward him because he brought me to the hospital?

My heart aches more than the limbs wrapped in casts. This hospital smells like formaldehyde. Just as formaldehyde preserves decaying things, smell acts like a preserving agent for memories. The hospital smell calls to mind this memory from last summer: It had been pouring since dawn. Half-asleep, I answered a phone call. I earnestly wished for an earthquake or war to erupt, to destroy everything between the moment I received the message and the moment I had to relay it to my father and the mother of my brother. My stepmother nagged me to tell her what the phone call was about. I could barely open my mouth to tell them. My father's mouth spilled the yogurt he was drinking. I passed out. I don't remember how we arrived at the hospital. I was bawling—I couldn't enter because of the repulsive smell. I cried outside. I didn't care if others thought I was overly dramatic. Fuck them. I preferred to jump off the Han River bridge than to look at my brother covered in a white sheet. Why couldn't I actually go through with that fantasy?

Hyunwoo, my stepbrother, and I were often asked if we were twins. We went to the same school and were in the same class level, but he was a quiet honor student and I was just another student. Strange rumors followed us. We commuted to school separately and ignored each other when we ran into each other in the hallway or the school yard. He was eight months younger than me, but never called me *nuna,* or big sister, and I didn't care about the secrets he so obviously was keeping. I often try to understand why I didn't kill myself when he died . . . or after. It feels shameful to keep on living. But sometimes I'm proud of myself and my life. My mind changes so much. It's like a pot of porridge that rapidly boils over and just as rapidly cools down. I feel addicted to my life, even if it's meaningless and degrading.

"Hohoho, you're awake! You must be hungry." A woman who looks like a doctor approaches my bed and then addresses a nurse. "It's been more than six hours since the surgery, right? Okay, bring her some porridge." The nurse adjusts the IV drip, and leaves the room. "Hohoho," the doctor laughs again. "Look at him. He is *out*." She bends down to shake the man in the low cot awake.

"Mother, leave me alone. Let me sleep ten more minutes!" the man complains. Then there's a thump as he falls off the cot—he must've tried to turn over. Grumbling, he stands up holding the side of my hospital bed and smiles at me. It's Jihyun, the dentist.

"When the nurse gets back with the porridge, you should eat a little, too," the doctor says to Jihyun. "And then get back to your office. This is *my* patient, you gotta tend to yours, hohoho." The doctor laughs at the end of each sentence.

Wait, did he call the doctor *mother*? Are they related? Are they a family of doctors?

"Yeoul? Is it okay if I just use your name?" The doctor asks me, laughing again. "You should've seen Jihyun when he brought you in. He was so upset. I don't know how he manages to operate on his patients. Well, you aren't too badly hurt, so think of this as an opportunity to get some rest. Let's get you some decent food, too. You seem malnourished. In this day and age, you shouldn't look like a war orphan! Since you are Jihyun's 'friend' and 'tutor,' you are our VIP at this hospital, okay? Hohoho."

"*Mother!* I think Yeoul needs some rest. You should go check on other patients. I'll take off in a little bit." The dentist uses a childish tone of voice to make his mother leave the room. "What do you think of my mother? Isn't she beautiful?" he asks once she's gone.

"Yes, she reminds me of Juliette Binoche," I reply.

"What a compliment! Did you guys make an arrangement to compliment each other or something? My mom said you are incredibly beautiful, too. She even asked, 'Don't she and I look like one another?' Haha."

"You're making stuff up to make me feel better."

"Well, be careful. My mother seems to be taken with you. She has . . . unusual taste."

"What do you mean?"

"Well . . . It's difficult to explain. Never mind."

The dentist asks me to call him by his first name, Jihyun, from now on. I don't really understand why everyone is dead set on finding the correct term of address for me to use. He asks me not to call him *Ajussi*, a middle-aged man, even though he is an unmarried bachelor. He'd prefer for me to use his name. He tells me he needs to get going, so he'll only be able to tell me the basics of how I got here, but that Eunyong and the café owner would be able to get into it with me. I think to myself, *I see, he doesn't want to talk about things that make him uncomfortable. He'll make the girls deal with it.*

"I didn't know you had such good reflexes!" Jihyun excitedly retells the story. "Even though you fell down the stairs with your arms tied behind the back, your neck is fine, and there isn't much injury. It's almost as though somebody caught you at the bottom of the stairs. It's extraordinary. Perhaps you should be showcased on TV. Yuri Geller the illusionist is not half as intriguing as your miracle!. Only one of your arms is broken, and a tendon in the leg is torn, which is no biggie." He suggests that I think of this miracle as a born-again type of fresh start that has been gifted to me. When will he stop talking? I'm bored, like I'm listening to some infomercial about a product I don't care about. But he continues rattling on. "The people in the billiard parlor all ran out to check out the commotion, and Eunyong called the café owner's place, but she wasn't there—she was out getting her hair permed—so my friend, her now-husband, answered and he called me. I rushed over, covered you with a blanket, took you to the hospital, and that brings us here." He laughs. "You were speaking gibberish on my back, so loudly too. I couldn't believe you actually were unconscious."

"Why is that so funny?" I pointedly ask him and his laughter fades. My face feels hot. Did I look funny being naked and unconscious? I hadn't bathed for a few days. How embarrassing. I want to ask about the monster, but I can't bring myself to talk about him, so instead I try moving my leg, and notice that my toenails are dirty. Ugh, so embarrassing. The hospital staff lady comes in with a tray of food, and Jihyun gets up to leave. He blows me a kiss, promising to stop by again that night. He's so annoying.

* * *

"What's your parents' phone number?" Eunyong insists on telling my father what happened. She looks worried.

The café owner interjects. "Why should we tell them though? Elders have weaker hearts, I don't want to surprise them. Let them assume no news is good news. Just visit them after you are discharged. I'm going to cover the hospital fee, so no need to worry your parents." This is the first time I've seen the café owner take a grave tone of voice. It disgusts me. She always acts like a child, only doing things that please her, but now she's taken on a serious tone, trying to perform the role of reasonable elder, but I see right through her. She's trying to control the situation to protect Sungyun, her nephew. I've been an idiot. Or was I pretending not to know? I shouldn't have thought she was a good person. Eunyong was right. She would've taken me to work at the sketchy bar in Guangan if she'd had her way.

"It was just a split-second bad decision," she sputters, "he must've been possessed or something. Must've been too drunk! Why else would he do such thing? I'm sorry. I apologize for him. I'll kneel before you if it'd please you."

"Do you know what Sungyun did to me? I wasn't the only one he did that kind of shit to either!" I bark back.

"Are you crazy? Do you want to ruin his life? He has been trying to be better. A man does that kind of stuff when he's drunk. Okay, let's be real. It's not like he got to *do it*. And he told me you invited yourself into his room!"

"What? Jesus Christ!"

"Sungyun called me and told me all about how it went down. You've been acting coy and distant, but I heard you went over to his place late that night and cried, asking for money? I told you I could pay you in advance if you were broke! You are so ungrateful to drag things out like this!" The irate café owner was screaming at me, before Eunyong finally intervened.

"Stop, stop! You didn't come here to fight with Yeoul! Yeoul, you should stop too."

The café owner turns to Eunyong. "Eunyong, you told me you want to marry Sungyun. So, let's set the date. But for now, just focus on taking care of the café, okay?"

"Umm, I thought I wanted that, but now, I'm not sure anymore. I want to think about it."

"You want to think about it? You *slept* with Sungyun. You slept with him so often your vagina must be all stretched out! I know you've been incessantly visiting him at night. So now what? Are you gonna pretend to be a virgin? Are you gonna try marrying someone else?"

The café owner huffed and puffed and demanded answers from us. It seemed like she wanted to waterboard us like secret service interrogators do to student protestors, until we gave her the answer she wanted. I'm more surprised that Eunyong kept this from me. I thought Eunyong just had a crush on Sungyun. I was going to let her know about what Hyunmi and I saw at the café that night when we caught him having sex. I didn't want to break her heart, so I put it off, but here we are. My stepmother used to yell at me—*You are so oblivious!* Perhaps she was right.

The café owner pulls Eunyong's arm to lead her out the door. "You are a mess, Sungyun won't be around for a while, so Eunyong will be busy taking care of the café. We won't be coming back. I guess I need to find another part-time girl. What a mess." Eunyong briefly turns to look at me, and her eyes are filled with tears.

I want to chuck the fruit basket the café owner brought right into the garbage can, but I can't move. I feel as stiff as a preserved frog floating in formaldehyde. And this smell. Can my own nose shrivel from the stench of my own body? *That bastard.* I hope my fury, my humiliation, my enmity against him won't deteriorate. I need them. The diaper someone put on me is soaked in urine. I might have shit a little too. I can't even clean myself. If that monster showed up with a knife right now, I wouldn't be able to fight back at all. He would be able to destroy me, to stab me. Considering what he's like, I could see him stabbing me hundreds of times. Would that be for the better? Which hole did he crawl into, where is he hiding?

Übermensch

The sun is setting between the birch trees. *It's beautiful*, I mumble without thinking. I wonder if I am inadvertently following the path of destiny set by some karmic fate. With a crutch under my arm I pace by the window. Considering the view of the birch forest, I guess I'm at the hospital that's on the top of the hill? I'm learning how to use the wheelchair, and the bandages are off, but for the last five days I haven't been able to move at all. I must have been drugged because I slept most of the time. But even when I was unconscious the voices were pestering me.

I asked the nurse to look out for me whenever unidentified men enter the hospital. I specified Jihyun to be the only man allowed into the room. I hope I won't have to use the crutch for self-defense.

Sol is here. She somehow heard about the whole thing. She keeps sighing, unlike her usual cheerful self. Her arms are crossed, and she doesn't say anything, just listens, which annoys me.

"I'm just worried you'll end up limping like me."

"That'd be fine with me. We can limp together." We laugh. Briefly the depression and agony disappear. I'll try to believe that it will stay that way.

Sol opens the book she brought and reads out loud. "'Up!' said he to himself, 'thou sleeper! Thou noontide sleeper! Well then, up, ye old legs! It's time and more than time; many a good stretch of road is still awaiting you. Now have ye slept your fill; for how long a time? A half-eternity! Well then, up now, mine old heart! For how long after such a sleep mayest thou remain awake?'"

"I know where that's from. *Thus Spoke Zarathustra*, right? You are like a mini-Jimin. Don't take it the wrong way though, it's supposed to be a compliment."

"I know. I hope you can shake off your demons, and rise up too." Sol presents her pinky finger, asking for a pinky promise. Without really knowing what I'm promising, I lift my right hand to hook my pinky to hers. I'm glad I still have fingers. Mini-Jimin pulls out a marker from the book. She came prepared for everything. Do you have a magic wand hidden somewhere in there too? She writes on the cast on my arm. My handwriting is terrible, but hers is even worse. Her scribble looks like a henna tattoo. It's nice. Übermensch.

"Do you know what this means?" Sol asks.

"Übermensch. A person who overcomes oneself. Superman." I answer, and she looks at me approvingly. "Hey, I majored in German. You're a Pharmaceutical major. Of course I know."

"Did you learn that kinda stuff from German professors? I don't think so. You learned it from Jimin didn't you?"

My heart darkens. Sol leaves and the room darkens too. I turn on the light but the corner of the room stays dark. She brought me a pen and a notebook, and I feel an urge to write something. What should I write? I've never had a day in my life when this many people came to see me. What if I just live here? What if I can stay unwell? They feed you, and friends visit you. Not bad.

Regardless, I am ailing in the hospital called the world. I write this line on the first page of the notebook. Not too bad for my own writing. Next, I'm going to write the list of people who visited me:

Kim Inja (Doctor/Jihyun's mom), Kim Sojung (nurse 1, skinny), Jeong Yunmi (nurse 2, wears a lot of makeup), Han Jihyun (visted twice), the lady who brings me meals (didn't catch her name, as old as my grandmother), Park Sol—

As I build this list, I am reminded of the list in that bastard's notebook and his belligerent response when I saw it. I'm pretty sure all the names on the list were women. What do those dates and names mean? I feel like I could make sense of it if I saw it one more time. Rapes? Murders? My imagination expands into the dark corners. I feel like if I don't stop myself I'm going to go crazy, kill myself, or kill someone. I desperately wait for slumber to arrive. I briefly fall asleep, and like a shadow, someone slips in through the door. I keep my eyes shut tight, feeling the gaze of a man by the bed. He runs his hand along my arm, bruised from needle marks. He pulls the blanket up to cover me and leaves something on the shelf by the bedside. I hear him walk to the window and picture him looking out. He returns to me, barely grazes my forehead with his fingertips, sighs, and slips back out of the room.

•

In my head, I heard a crow flying, *caw caw.*

I was about seven years old, crying, and as the sun was going down, I looked up at the sky above my grandma's fence. An unfamiliar lady gave me a small carton of milk, gently brushed my forehead with her hand, and left.

After he'd gone, I struggle to get up and look at what he left behind. A bottle of cherry juice, a carton of strawberry milk, straws, two tangerines, and a poetry book by Baudelaire. I didn't know a dentist could be this nice. It's so late at night too. It's almost creepy that he made a point to come by.

I pull the spout of the milk carton open, put the straw in, and suck the milk through the straw. Is a mother's milk supposed to be as tasty as this? Was I ever breastfed? In the silent stillness of the night, I fall asleep with the milk carton in my hand.

Metamorphosis

A detective stops by.

"So what happened was . . ." I stumble over my words as I try to explain what happened, what Sungyun did to me. The detective chuckles as he takes his hat off. Shit, I realize it's the bastard. He pulls a gun out of his belt and presses the barrel against my temple. The gunshot rings in the air.

"Are you there?" The door opens and Jihyun wakes me up from the dream.

"You scared me."

Jihyun commutes here nearly every day. There were a few days he couldn't make it, but as if he wanted to make up for those days, he visited several times on other days. "You'll be discharged tomorrow. It's a good thing, but I almost feel sad that I won't be able to find you here anymore." He trails off, and pulls out a CD from the inner pocket of his jacket. He opens the CD player—he got it for me for my stay in this room—and gently places the CD into the slot. Last night, he shared that he actually wanted to major in music, but his mother was fiercely against the idea, so he went to study dentistry. He said he's sick of looking into the mouths of strangers every day. He said he'd like to play his electric guitar for me and added that since the hospital room wasn't a good place for that, I would have to come over to his place—I couldn't tell if he was joking or serious. The music he put on feels dark. Sounds like . . . progressive rock?

"They're a Sicilian art-rock band. They were active in the Italian underground scene. After releasing albums in 1972 and 1973, they disappeared like a ghost. This is their second album. Pretty good, huh?"

"It's a little depressing and monotonic, but mesmerizing. What's the band's name?"

"Their band name means *Byeontae*, it means . . ."

I interrupt. "Eek, what?"

"Haha, no, not the perverted *byeontae*. *Byeontae*—transformation. Their name is Metamorfosi."

At the end of the sentence, we both get noticeably sadder. The cover image of the album looks like the hell from Dante's *Inferno*.

"I did a background check on Sungyun . . . He has several criminal charges of attempted rape. He's paid a million won in fines. There were a bunch of other cases he tried to settle with the women . . . His reputation among the vendors in the neighborhood is not good. What do you plan to do after you're discharged?"

"I feel conflicted. A few days ago, my friends stopped by, including Sol, and we were discussing what we should do after I'm discharged. My Sunbe's suicide also seems to be linked to him, and I feel like I shouldn't just sit around and do nothing. I'm a little scared. I'm not sure what to do. Do you know where he is?"

"The rumor is that he ran off to the countryside, or that

he's lying low somewhere nearby. Is hanging out with your friends from the Blue Stockings a good idea? Isn't that dangerous? It's not just Sungyun you'd be dealing with. He's a part of Onchun-2-dong, that group of gangsters. It's going to be tough, but . . ."

"But?"

"I might be being nosy. I admit I have no idea what's going on in your family, but what do you think about moving back with your parents? Just make up with them? After staying there for a while, you can move out once we get married . . . If we hurry, we can make it happen fast."

"Wait, *doctor*. I'm really grateful you brought me here and that you've been helping me. But what are you talking about? Where is this coming from? I think you have some unexamined assumptions, no, fantasies about women, marriage, and starting a family."

"Why are you suddenly addressing me as *doctor*? I'm just trying to figure out how to protect you, how to make you happy. I haven't dated much, so I don't really know women. I don't have siblings, nor many friends or cousins, so I don't know much about women. I admit it. I just want to be with someone I can talk to and listen to music with, someone I can be true friends with. Please don't misunderstand what I'm trying to say."

"Okay, I'll call you Jihyun. Jihyun, you're nine years older than me. Why do you use the honorific with me? Why haven't you even touched my hand if you're interested in me? A lot of things you say don't make sense to me. Is this marriage talk coming from some sort of weird sense of ethical obligation after carrying me while I was naked?"

"One question at a time, please. What am I supposed to do if you carpet-bomb me like that?" He forces a laugh before responding. "Okay, let me answer . . . What was your first question? Okay. So you are saying I can talk to you casually, right? Well, I'd like that." He switches the phrasing with me and continues. "Secondly, why don't I even touch your hand? Well . . ." He looks at my fingers. My nails are a mess from my nail-biting habit. I curl my fingers to hide them. He gently places his hand over mine. I can feel the lines of his palms. They feel like they will leave marks on the back of my hand. He has a warm, soft hand. Unlike mine, there are no hard calluses. Jihyun takes his dress shoes off, crawls onto the bed, and lies down by my side. I no longer wait for a kiss with my eyes closed like the time before. I lean in to kiss him. I want more. More. More.

Is what I'm doing some sort of stubborn protest, a demand for love? Does this have anything to do with the fact that he looks like my father? Ugh, I don't know. Why are his lips so much sweeter and softer than Hyunmi's? After our lips part, he smiles shyly. He strokes my cheek, and then kisses my forehead. He reaches his arm around me and pats me on the back.

"Yeoul, I want to fall asleep with you in my arms. I feel like we will rise up and float in the air. This feels like a dream. Once you are discharged, let's go on a gondola ride. No, not the one in the amusement park, but the real gondola in Venice . . ."

Knock knock knock. The doctor walks in with her hands full of shopping bags. She looks like some rich lady who loves shopping just getting back from her favorite department store. The hands of the clock on the wall are pointing eleven o'clock. "Yeoul, what are you doing staying up with the lights on this late?" Her wide eyes gleam. "And you!" she says to Jihyun, "Weren't you here earlier today? What are you still doing here? Do you plan on going to work tomorrow? Go home. She needs to rest too! Lying in bed with the patient, how professional. Some doctor you are!"

"Speaking of professionalism, Mom, what are you doing visiting here in the middle of the night?"

"What? I was going to stop by tomorrow, and I saw the lights. Yeoul, I thought you wouldn't have clothes to wear when you are discharged tomorrow, so I brought you some things. They'll probably fit you." She opens the shopping bag, inside is a pair of Jordache jeans, a cool T-shirt with skull patterns, a pair of sneakers. Everything looks super trendy. They must be expensive, the kind even rich kids have a hard time affording.

After she's shown me everything, she goes back to her fake scolding tone. "Yeoul, go to sleep. Jihyun, get down from the bed. It's cramped! Come on. Go home and sleep in your own bed." It's hard to tell if Jihyun and his mom care for each other given the way they are at each other like cats and dogs. The doctor nags him a little more, and then whispers to me, "Before you leave the hospital tomorrow, stop by at my office. I have something I have to tell you." She says it with such gravity, I wonder what it could be.

After she's left the room, Jihyun awkwardly climbs down from the bed. "Is there something going on between you and my mom?" he asks.

I think to myself, *What a strange question*, and reply, biting into a crispy apple: "What kind of question is that? And what's up with your mom? It's nice of her that she got me all these things, but it's a bit much."

"It's hard to explain, or maybe it's not so hard. Oh shoot, I said I wouldn't use the honorific, but here I am again. *Okay,*" he switches back to casual. "My parents are separated. My dad lives in Italy. He's a tour guide for the Korean tourists, and also a professor of music. Voice, to be specific. He rides his boats everywhere. Mom says he's stricken with wanderlust."

"When did your parents separate?"

"As soon as I got into university. So it's been a while. My mom had an affair with a movie director, someone my father knew too. And the director was . . . a woman. Does that surprise you?"

"So you're saying, the person your mother fell in love with was a woman?" I've never heard anyone say this out loud.

"Yeah, they couldn't live without each other, or so I heard. This is the first time I've talked about this. I can't tell anyone, how am I supposed to explain this kind of situation? Do I just say my mom is . . . a *lesbian*? How do I make sense of things like that for myself and others? I have no word. I guess the correct term would be . . . *bisexual*?" He covers his face with his hands, and his shoulders shake. He looks like a distressed adolescent. No, a child. I get up from the bed and walk around him to pat his back from behind. I open my arms, wrap my arms around his curled-up-body, and pull him into my chest. It's like I've become a mama bird nesting her egg. A sob jumps out of my mouth unexpectedly. We are thinking of different things, but we are crying together. When our tears stop and our eyes slowly open, will we find ourselves different from before? Will we be able to love each other as we have become—these new images of each other?

I feel a light come on inside my body. I get a glimpse of where to go next. Why couldn't I have thought like this before? I limp out with Jihyun. We kiss in the elevator. I smell formaldehyde from his lips. He touches my leg. He tells me I need to keep using my crutch after the discharge (which is in a few hours), even if it's uncomfortable. After he leaves, I turn to face the quiet corridor. The sound of my footsteps reverberates in the air. I catch myself trying not to step on the lines between the square tiles as I hobble. I dunno. What the hell. I'm just following my crutch as it leads me on. Where are you going? Where are you taking me? Are you taking me to the rooftop so I can jump off? Are you going to have me kill myself before I can kill that bastard? Coward. I've been asking myself these questions all day. The dark corridor never comes to an end. I stop at the open door with a plaque that reads HOSPITAL DIRECTOR, KIM INJA.

The doctor welcomes me in. "I was about to head out. Sit, sit. Did Jihyun head home?"

"Yes."

"I was going to talk to you tomorrow, but since you are here now . . ."

"There's no tomorrow for me."

"Hohoho."

Why is she always so cheerful? I feel small and pathetic.

She touches my hair like I'm Juliet Binoche from *The Unbearable Lightness of Being,* or *Mauvais Sang,* or *Le Rayon Vert.* I feel like I've known this woman for a long time. I like her short hair, her long legs. I like her voice, her laugh, and her smell . . . my leg aches.

"Yeoul, Yeoul, Yeoul . . . Jeong Yeoul."

"Yes?"

"Yeoul, when your mother was naming you, I was there. I tried to steer her away from the name. I thought it wasn't a good name for a baby. *Yeoul,* rapids, the rocky part of the river where the water is rough, is hard to paddle through, and I worried naming you that way would make your life a rough one."

"What are you talking about? Oh, I see, you're kidding. Don't joke about things like that."

The hospital director hands me a folded piece of paper. "Go to this address." She says. "The person you miss lives there."

What? Why is she speaking nonsense? What? . . . All I hear is static noise, *Pssssssst.* I turn the dial but keep missing the radio signal . . .

. . . We now speak in an alien language, one from the Andromeda galaxy. I'm stranded in this universe. A train cuts through the darkness and crosses the Milky Way to arrive. Hello Galaxy Express,[8] I grin as I get on the train. I chuck

8. *Galaxy Express 999* is an animated sci-fi series broadcast in Korea during the 1980s. The series follows an orphan boy traveling to the Andromeda galaxy on a space-train called the Galaxy Express 999. He runs into Maetel, a woman who looks exactly like his dead mother.

the crutch into the night sky. We need to kill the cyborgs, need to save Maetel from the villains, and . . . Even in my fantasy I'm being hounded by things I must do. *Shut up, shut up*! Stop making things up as if my life were a kid's cartoon.

Hey Hey Hey

"How are you? Isn't it nice to be out of the hospital? Congratulations!" Jihyun seems elated as if he were the one who just got released.

I take a step back like a piece of glass was kicked up into my face. "The sun feels super bright."

"It feels good though, right?" Jihyun touches my face, and lightly hugs me.

"Yes." Deep breath. The air is fresher out here. The wind is blowing.

"The wind is rising. We must try to live." Jimin said on one windy day.

"That was pretty, Sunbe, what you just said." I watched Jimin's face, feeling full of love and admiration for her. She seemed embarrassed at the sight of my enthusiasm and curtly replied, "That's from a Paul Valéry poem. I can't take credit for that."

"Regardless, I like it."

Regardless, the wind is rising. Ah, I want to live, I'm going mad with the desire to live madly. When I push open the door to exit the hospital, I'm no longer the same me from yesterday. The wind blows away those tangled threads of thoughts that I had woven, unwoven, and woven again, and while I'm absorbing my surroundings a sleek black car pulls into the hospital's gate, so close that it almost hit me, and comes to a stop. A man exits the driver's side, and walks around to open the rear door—shiny high heels emerge first, then black stockinged legs, then a violet skirt—a woman in a fancy outfit gets out.

"Oh? Jihyun! So good to see you. How are you do—" The woman pauses midsentence and scans me.

"Oh, hi Yuna." Jihyun replies, "What brings you here? Are you feeling sick?"

"No," she laughs, "I'm fine. Just visiting my cousin. Good to see you. Let's grab coffee sometime."

"Yes, let's." Jihyun opens the door for the woman as she brings her fist to her ear, her thumb and her pinky extended, gesturing him to call her sometime. She unfurls her hand and waves before she enters.

"Who's that?"

"Someone I had a blind date with last year."

"She's so pretty. Is she Miss Korea or something?"

"Actually, yes."

"Whoa."

I notice a man holding a cigarette in his lips. He lifts his chin in my direction, and a man next to him crumples a paper cup in his hand and throws it to the ground. They watch me intently. I feel paranoid. Maybe they were just checking out the woman who went into the hospital. Today, I coach myself, I'm not going to try predicting the future. Not gonna try anything stupid. Please. The wind is rising today.

Jihyun holds my hand with one of his and pulls my suitcase with the other, guiding me to the parking lot. Early in the morning he arrived at the hospital, pulled out all the stuff I'd been keeping in paper bags, and transferred them gently into the suitcase. Now he opens the trunk of his car.

"Yeoul, Yeoul!" It's Sol and Eunyong, running over to me with their shirts billowing behind them. They each hold plastic bags full of stuff with the name of the supermarket. When they reach us, they are huffing and puffing. The beads of sweat on Sol's forehead reflect the sun and glisten; it feels like they should make the sounds of jingling bells. Eunyong speaks: "We almost missed you leaving! You were gonna take off before we got here, just like that?" I can't tell if she's teasing or genuinely hurt. "Well, this is your stuff from your old place. Your clothes and books. We packed them up for you." Only then does she really see me. "Wait. You look nice. Where did you get the new clothes?" Eunyong makes me twirl to see my clothes from all directions.

"Well, the hospital director insisted . . ."

"Huh. So you're like her new daughter-in-law or something?" Eunyong turns to Jihyun and comfortably addresses him. "Hello. We've met. I'm Yeoul's friend."

"Of course I remember. No need to reintroduce yourself."

Sol watches me in silence.

★ ★ ★

"The wind is blasting in my face back here. Close the window!" Eunyong breaks the awkward silence in the car. Jihyun has been driving, stiffly looking ahead, never turning his gaze anywhere else even when we were at a red light. But at Eunyong's complaint, he briefly glances at the back seat through the mirror.

"Sol, why are you so quiet? Are you upset or something?"

"No, I'm just tired from sprinting earlier."

Eunyong interrupts, "Why didn't you wait for me? Did you think we weren't gonna show up on the day you get to leave the hospital? It's a day to celebrate!"

"I waited for you to come all morning. I thought you guys couldn't make it, so that's why we were taking off . . . Hey, I want to show you guys something later."

"What is it?"

"A piece of paper that I got . . . It might be a letter. I want us to read it together later." I turn away from the back seat, holding the folded piece of the doctor gave me, and through the mirror I watch Sol, very still, with her gaze fixated somewhere beyond the window.

"Let's all go out for lunch together." Jihyun suggests, "I made a reservation at a restaurant. How does that sound? It's on me, of course."

"Hurray! I thought we were going to have some cheap rice cake or gimbap roll at a snack bar. Thanks!" Eunyong claps with overexcitement.

There aren't any good places to park, so Jihyun loops around the restaurant a few times and parks somewhere down the back alley, pulling up close to the brick fence. "We're a bit far from the restaurant. Are you okay to walk?" When Jihyun tries to help me out of the car after taking my crutch out of the trunk, Sol grabs my hand, tightly interlaces her fingers with mine, and leads me away from him.

"I'm feeling fine. Really." I lift my right leg to prove it.

There's a beautiful courtyard at the restaurant. Fish as large as a man's forearm languidly swim in the pond. A pathway framed by cedar trees leads us to the restaurant, and several servers respectfully bow at Jihyun. He whispers something to the man who looks like the restaurant's manager, and we are led to a large room with windows framed with elegant geometric patterns.

"First, we'll get five servings of ribeye, and when we are almost done with the meat, please bring in the bamboo rice and miso soup." Jihyun continues, "and three large bottles of beer. Anything else?"

"I have a class today, so I can't drink. And I don't particularly care for meat." Sol says curtly, as she pulls her jacket off her arm.

Eunyong pokes her in the waist. "Don't complain. He's the one who's buying!" The two of them seem to have become friends while visiting me at the hospital.

As the night goes on, we keep ordering extra meat. By the end of the night, we have finished nine servings, but we didn't eat that much. Each "serving" was about the size of my palm, and technically speaking, there aren't four of us eating here. There are five. Eunyong scrapes the grill attached to the table with her spoon to get the charred bits of meat. I tell her to stop. "Eunyong, don't eat that. Don't you know you have to eat only pretty things when you are pregnant? Otherwise, you have an ugly kid."

Eunyong's showing. Her belly is sticking out, and the hormonal freckles are spreading across her face.

"You're pregnant?" Jihyun pauses on his way to the cashier and sits back down.

"Heh . . ." Eunyong awkwardly laughs.

"Whose is it? How long has it been? How could you? You aren't married!"

"Stop asking so many questions! I haven't even told my mom. The café owner is nagging me to get an abortion, telling me Sungyun isn't coming back. But then my obstetrician told me it's too late for an abortion. You're a doctor. What do *you* think? Everybody is scolding me, and scaring me, telling me that I've made the worst mistake, and that I'll forever be a single mom, everybody will point their fingers at me. I was even told to check myself into the single-mom facility! I was told international adoption would be a good option. Well, Sol, you're the one who told me about that. How many kids are adopted abroad again?"

"Since the end of the Korean War, about 140,000 kids have been adopted abroad. But that's just according to the government survey, so I bet there are more."

"Wait, wait. Are you considering giving away your child?" Jihyun frowns as though he is looking at a criminal accused of a heinous crime.

"She never said she was committed to that idea. I was just educating this mother-to-be about her options. We've been talking about the reality of things, the limited options available to women in this position, how to be a resilient mom, given the circumstances. Who knows what the right choice will be?" Sol shrugs.

Suddenly Eunyong starts bawling. "What am I supposed to do? What am I going to do with the baby when he arrives? I want to have the baby. Please help me find Sungyun."

Sol is mortified. Jihyun leaves the room to pay the cashier for the meal.

I put my hand over Eunyong's mouth. "Are you crazy? Everybody can hear you." My hand gets soaked in her tears and snot. She starts coughing, the way Nana did when she swallowed something wrong and I had to put my finger down her throat to get it out. "Stop crying, Eunyong. You idiot. The world isn't going to end, I promise. Everything will be okay. You have me. I'm here for you, okay?" I try to comfort her, taking on a confident tone and tapping my chest, but my chest feels tight like I've swallowed something wrong. Like Eunyong, I want to find Sungyun too, but for a very different reason. But what would I do if I find Sungyun? I hate him so much I don't know what I'd do. Eunyong, my friend, is pregnant with his baby. If she actually delivers the baby, how will I feel? "Alright, we're supposed to be celebrating me being discharged from the hospital today, right? Then I say, let's go somewhere. That'll make all of us feel better. And you will be making my wish come true."

"What are your wishes?" Eunyong asks. Her face is still red from crying, but she is now smiling.

"Taking a road trip."

"That's your wish?"

"Yes."

★ ★ ★

"Alright, my princesses. Where shall we go now?" Jihyun asks from the driver's seat. He is smiling, but his smile is vacant. I think he's still in shock from Eunyong's emotional outburst.

"Don't you need to head back to work?" I ask.

"Well, I closed the office today. I posted a note that I had to go take a dentistry seminar."

"You must be a good liar. Do you lie often?"

"Nope. But for you I will."

"Ugh, cheesy!" Sol and Eunyong make gagging noises from the back seat. Without turning around, I can see the faces they are making. I feel nauseated too.

"Less lying, more driving." Eunyong adds from the back seat.

"Well, I can't start driving unless you decide on the destination."

"Let's get out of town. Taejong Beach, I heard it's hard to get there by public transportation. Let's go there." Sol readily makes this suggestion, she must have thought about going there before.

I hesitate. "That's in the Youngdo District . . ."

"What? You don't like Youngdo?"

"No. I've been thinking about going to Youngdo. I'm just surprised that you and I are on the same page. I felt like you read my mind."

"Is that right? Cool, telepathy!" Sol smiles her pretty smile for the first time today.

"But Sol, you said you have a class today, right?" I ask.

"I'm already late for it anyway. Whatever. Don't worry about it."

"Aren't you worried about the class? I thought that's why you were being moody."

"No, it's just . . . I've got a lot on my plate."

"Like what?"

"I'm having a hard time keeping up with course loads, the Feminist Students' Association is falling apart, one Sunbe is harassing me to join his band, but most of all: you, you troublemaker. And you, Ms. Preggers. You guys give me a headache."

Sol points at Eunyong, and Eunyong protests. "What have I done? Yeoul is constantly stirring stuff up, but I didn't do anything." She changes the topic, "Anyway, do you know there's a huge boulder at Taejong Beach that people keep throwing themselves off of? It got so bad that the city council had to post a sign to discourage suicide."

Jihyun asks, "What does the sign say?"

"I heard it says, *Citizens, please think it over!*"

"That's stupid," I sneer. I'm getting sleepy.

"I heard a funny story about the boulder." Jihyun offers. "One day, this guy climbed the suicide boulder to kill himself, right? But then, when he looked down from the boulder and saw how tall it was, he got scared. It was a stormy day, and he turned around to try to get out of there. But then what did he see? The sign: *Think it over!* So he thought it over, and threw himself off the boulder."

Only Jihyun laughs. He glances at me, so I make a half-hearted snort.

"Alright. To Taejong Beach!" Jihyun turns the music on,

and grabs the steering wheel. The sound of the guitar suddenly penetrates and shatters me.

Hey Jude, don't make it bad.
Take a sad song and make it better.
Remember to let her into your heart.
Then you can start to make it better.

Someone once told me that the book on someone's bedside table reveals a lot about the person—their tastes, but also the mental space they're in. Perhaps Jihyun—based on this song—is dreaming of a simple, conventional life. He might always have been that way. It's a good thing, I think, to listen to a popular song and be able to feel something. That means you are part of the larger world, the majority of people. I want that life—it's a simple, pleasant way to live.

Listening to this song, I wonder, is Jihyun also afraid of letting "her" into his heart? Could that "her" be me? I hope he realizes that he is being stupid, acting so cool and nonchalant toward me. He might already know.

I wonder whether Hyunwoo thought of me as "her."

Before he and I were estranged we used to listen to The Beatles together. We were in middle school then. He used to sing "Hey Jude," his favorite song that he could actually sing. When the song reached the part that is playing right now—"Better better better, OH!"—he sang along with his eyes clenched shut, building up to the high pitch by screaming, playing air guitar along with the music. He was usually so withdrawn. Making those big movements while blasting the loud music through his headphone was the best he could do to let himself loose. When I told him my favorite Beatle was John Lennon, not Paul McCartney, he said he used to feel that way too but not anymore. I should have granted him his wishes. If I had, would he still be alive?

My stepbrother, Hyunwoo. It's weird to think to him in the role of brother. Is that who he was to me? *Brother?* Today I keep catching myself thinking about him. I find myself thinking about him whenever I decide that I, in fact, want to live. Or when I'm tasting something delicious and want to share it with him, or when I decide to leave where I am for somewhere else. No, I'll be honest. I don't know if there is a pattern to my thoughts. He keeps popping up in my mind regardless of time and space and now, with Jimin gone, they take turns appearing. I feel responsible for their deaths. I am a killer. I murdered the two people I loved most last year alone. So I sing to myself:

> *Hey Yeoul, don't you dare dream*
> *You have no right to enjoy your life.*
> *No way, no way, no way, oh.*

Plastic Fish

The road before us forks. We pause, deciding which way to take. The path on the left is lined with flowering trees, the trees sprinkled with fuzzy magnolia flower buds and red camellias. On the right leads to the ever-widening sea. One of us makes an unusual suggestion of splitting up to explore both ways, and we learn that both ways are part of the same loop that lead back to the same spot. We start walking toward the sea. A few people are jogging. A middle-aged man in a form-fitting yellow jumpsuit with a black stripe down the side stares at us as he jogs by.

"Does he think he's Bruce Lee or something? What kind of outfit's that? Why is he staring at us?" Eunyong grumbles. My right leg limps, Sol's left leg limps, Eunyong's belly balloons under her chocolate-colored shirt (which reminds me of Nana's fur), and a man in a clean suits walks beside us. We add up to a strange assembly. No wonder the man stared. My head feels heavy. I want a cigarette.

"Keep going. I'll catch up after getting myself a pack of cigarettes."

As I turn around, Jihyun shakes his hand to stop me. "I think I saw a convenience store next to the ticketing office.

That shop is too far back. You shouldn't walk that far. Can't you hold off? Smoking is bad for you anyway."

"No, I can't hold off. I gotta have one."

"Okay then. I'll go get it for you."

Watching Jihyun running back to the shop, Sol speaks with a sneer. "Even though he pretends to negotiate with you, he always ends up doing what you want."

"What are you talking about?"

"Anyway. How does it feel to come back from near-death?" Sol changes the tune.

"I'm feeling tired," I admit.

Sol points. "Let's sit there for now."

There's a little garden with some sort of monument, and we sit on its marble platform. A squirrel is startled by us. The platform is cold, so I turn to tell Sol to sit on my lap, but she sits on the rock across from me.

"Are you going to his place tonight? Are you moving in with him?" Sol asks abruptly and urgently, as though she's been holding back this question, waiting for this moment.

"I dunno."

"Are you guys officially dating now? You guys even dropped the honorific, I guess you really are going to live together, huh?"

"I really don't know. Stop saying things as though they're decided."

"If you aren't moving in with him, why else did he buy all that stuff?"

"What stuff?"

"I saw him buying several packages of frozen bone

broth from the restaurant earlier. It's supposed to be good for bones, right? He's clearly thinking about feeding you."

"I didn't know about any of that."

"I don't like how you're all, *I dunno, I dunno.* You seem so passive. Even defeated! Yeah, I know you've been struggling, and yeah, things are rough. But are you just gonna go with him like you're a piece of gum that got stuck to his shoe?"

"Is that how you think of me? You don't take me or my life seriously!" I'm pissed and I jump up to my feet.

Eunyong, who's been staying out of the conversation, minding her own business in the distance, comes back to intervene. "Whoa, my friends. Please don't fight. If you want to fight, at least make it physical, grab each other's hair, make it fun. Don't do it like this." Eunyong is in a good mood for some reason and picks a flower from the bush, pins it to her hair, and giggles to herself. She stops giggling when she walks up to the monument and reads its plaque: "'On December 24th 1970, four men from the Army Corps, Construction Unit 1203, died in an accident while blasting the cliff to build this road.' Fuck. They were working the soldiers on Christmas Eve? Sheesh!" Eunyong's brother is in the army, which might be why she's upset by it. Somehow I sense that there might be more to her sudden fury.

"Here." Jihyun is back and hands me the pack of cigarettes. I open it, but then feel too awkward to smoke in front of the monument. It seems disrespectful. I don't want my cigarette smoke to bother these poor men's souls. When I put the pack of cigarettes into my pocket, I find the letter I'd been meaning to read.

"Read this for me," I pass the piece of paper that I folded up in the shape of a kite to Sol.

"What is this? Is this for me? Should I read it now?"

"No, let's go to the lookout point first. I saw on the map there are coffee shops and an observatory up there. Let's read it there."

Unlike in the movies, walking along the winter beach is not very romantic. It's too cold, and my shoulders are shivering. Jihyun takes my hand and guides our hands into his pocket. His persimmon-colored jacket is soft and smooth. I suddenly feel a small, malleable object in his pocket.

"Eek, what's that?" I jerk my hand out of his pocket, and Jihyun pulls out a plastic orange goldfish.

"Huh? You bought a fish?"

"The supermarket had it. I thought it was cute. I promise: I will always be at your side until this fish comes to life and swims." Jihyun acts like a little boy confessing his love and turns bright red. I didn't see this coming.

"What's going on over here?" Eunyong snatches the fish out of my hand and tosses it up and down, throwing it higher than her head. "What's this? A plastic goldfish? I guess that's cool. Wish you bought us some fish-waffles instead."

Jihyun jumps up and down to take the fish back from Eunyong. "You give that back, and I'll get the fish-waffles or whatever you're talking about. Do they sell it in the bakery?"

"You're too rich to know anything about street food, hm? I'm sure you can't even tell fish-waffles from flower-waffles." Eunyong sticks her tongue out and runs off with the toy in her hand. Jihyun pursues her.

Why does he like me? Does he think we live in some

kind of fantasy land where plastic fish swim in the pond, and toy soldiers shake hands with elephants, and he is a prince on a white horse rescuing the damsel in distress? The seagulls flock in distance, and the sea is calm. I'm like an injured fish that needs to spend a night in his safe aquarium. Tonight would be that night.

Crossword Puzzle

We arrive at the lookout point with the observatory. Instead of looking out to appreciate the landscape in awe (or confusion), Eunyong looks up into the wide-open sky. The sky is empty, and I suddenly feel like it matches my prospects. Sol puts a coin into the binocular stand's coin slot and presses her eyes against the viewfinder. All there is to see is the ocean and the clouds. Sol always seems to be interested in the things that one can't see with the naked eye, she wants to see more, to look under the surface.

I restlessly pace around the observatory and run into a large sculpture at the center of the lookout point. The sculpture takes the shape of a mother holding a child in her arms, and you can trace the visitors' touch by the hand marks. It's hard to tell what kind of face the mother is making. It's not sculpted delicately, so it's not very detailed. Or perhaps the worms of time slowly ate away her pupils, nose, neck, and fingers. I feel an odd sensation of déjà vu. I feel like I've seen this mother–child sculpture before. I'm certain that I have. But this is my first time in Taejong Beach. Am I confusing that sculpture with Michelangelo's *Pieta*, which I'm obsessed with? It can't be. The woman doesn't look anything like Mary, or the son like Jesus. Where did I see this sculpture before?

We follow the arrows pointing to the lighthouse coffee shop. The arrows guide us to climb down a spiral staircase leading to the basement. The place looks like an old tea shop. The lights are dim, and melodramatic Teuroteu music is playing. The miniskirt-clad clerk greets us.

"Do you have mango juice?" Eunyong asks.

"We only have orange juice."

Eunyong orders juice anyway and the rest of us order hot cocoa.

"Sol, could you read the letter I gave you? Out loud so we all can read it together. The hospital director gave it to me."

Sol unfolds the paper that I folded tight, and reads the letter sing-songily:

Dear Yeoul,

It was hard to be stuck in the hospital for a week, wasn't it? You will be discharged tomorrow. I'm so glad you are recovering well. Even after you're released, don't forget to come every Wednesday to be tested and to get meds, okay? I told Dr. Yoon to take special care of you, so if you think you'll need physical therapy or need to consult with anyone, go to him. You'll be done with the cast in no time as long as you walk regularly.

I'm flying to Verona tomorrow. Jihyun's father is feeling very ill. When he describes the symptoms to me, I suspect he might have stomach cancer, but he is a stubborn man and won't go to see a doctor. Jihyun wants to spend a few more days in Korea before visiting him—I think he cares about you a lot. I wonder how you feel about him. I don't mind if you decide to stay with him at our place for a while. I trust you two.

Yeoul. I think of you as my own daughter. I was there when you were born. You were born prematurely, and it was a difficult delivery. When you were an infant, I took care of you; when you cried, I comforted you. You were a lovely little crybaby. Despite this past and our fateful connection, I didn't actively look for you until you arrived at the hospital. Even then I didn't immediately recognize you. I'm sorry. You've grown up strong and beautiful, perhaps more so than people whose parents looked after them. I believe that some sort of Presence has been looking out for you. I don't know much about the Mystery and all that, but your mother always talks about the power of prayer.

Your mother and I were best friends in middle and high school. Your mother was the prettiest and smartest girl in the town of Masan. On the street passersby would turn to stare at her, that's how pretty she was. It's all in the past, I suppose. I went to college in Seoul, but your family was financially struggling, so your mother couldn't. My parents offered to lend some money to your family for the tuition, but your grandfather didn't allow her to take the offer, so she stayed in the town, took care of the family. Not long after, your grandfather didn't come back after sailing out into the ocean. I don't believe that your mother's life was held back by her father or husband. She said she was happy, happier than most people. She told me she loved her life. I haven't seen her *since Christmas two years ago, but I'd like to think that everything is going well for her. No news is good news. My best friend, your mother, is a proud woman and she never reaches out first. Other than how distant she can get, your mother has a perfect personality. Not having been in touch with her, I haven't gotten around to telling her that I coincidentally and miraculously met you, or about your hospitalization, or your relationship with my son. I'm curious how she'd react, but I'm not sure it's my place to be the first one to tell her.*

I wanted to tell you all this in person, but it's hard to talk about it, so I wrote you a letter. Sorry about the smudges on the letter. I'm feeling a little emotional. I hope you understand how I feel. I'm including your mother's address and I hope you two can catch up. I love you.

Busan, Yeongdo District, Sinsun, San 58-4. Gang Jinae.

—1988 March 5th, Inja Kim.

Upon finishing the letter we grow silent, and the ambient sounds grow louder. The café's crappy sound system plays an old song, and it sounds like mice are gnawing on something in the ceiling while the singer sings.

Life moves on like a traveler, a cloud—goes on without a refuge. Life, we all arrive empty-handed and naked . . .

I've heard this song before. Is this the song my pathetic father sang when he was drunk?

"This is crazy. So your doctor turned out to be your

missing mother's best friend? Is a coincidence like this actually possible?" Sol mumbles as though she's asking herself.

"I can't believe it either," my voice is barely audible.

"The address is near here. Are you gonna go see your mom?" Sol presses on.

"Dunno."

"You've been all, *I dunno, I dunno* this whole time. Did you get a concussion when you fell down the stairs?"

"What do you want from me? I don't know what I should do!"

"Have you ever met her before?"

"Who?"

"Your mom, of course."

"I haven't seen her since she took off. I don't even remember what she looks like. And I think the woman she's speaking of isn't my mom."

"What?"

"Gang Jinae. That's not my mom's name."

"Huh?"

"My mom's name is Jongok. Gang Jongok. I know that much."

"Then . . . is this whole thing her confusing you with someone else?"

"Maybe."

"Ahh! This is too confusing. I don't know what to make of all this. Gimme that again." Sol reads over the letter, mumbling to herself.

"Um," Jihyun starts tentatively, "I'm pretty sure the Gang Jinae my mom writes of *is* your mom. My mother isn't the kind of person to make hasty conjectures." He pauses, as if weighing whether to go on. "She and I talked about this last night, and I'm convinced she got it right. About the name not being different . . . well, think about it. Nobody gets the name one chooses, so some people change their name when they feel like they've changed. The poet Kim Sowol changed his name. He was originally Kim Jongshik, and the poet Yi Yuksa, that name isn't his original name, either. There's a chance that Yeoul's mother changed her name too." Jihyun speaks like a gentle high school teacher, gazing deeply into our eyes.

"Are you just guessing all that? Or did your mom say something about Yeoul's mom changing her name?" Sol asks.

"No, she didn't say anything about that when we talked. She just told me she is friends with Yeoul's mom, and that that's why she was so nice to Yeoul. This letter is new to me, too. So maybe I don't know what I'm talking about. It's unusual for my mom to tell me anything about her life— we barely eat together, each of us being so busy and all." All our faces darken. Maybe even if I had known my mother I wouldn't really know her.

We face the letter gravely, as though we will only be released from it if we navigate its twisted maze, solve this crossword puzzle. I didn't mean to bring us down like this, but I couldn't face the letter on my own. My head aches. It feels like worms writhing inside my skull are trying to find their way out. I've been feeling achy and obsessive ever since I received the letter last night.

Eunyong suddenly claps loudly and announces, "Alright, alright, cheer up, you guys. Nothing's that complicated here. Let's go to this address and fact-check! What, this isn't like

3000 Leagues in Search of Mother. We're so close, and the address is right here in front of us." Eunyong has seemed changed ever since she got pregnant—she used to sneak food from the kitchen like a little girl and slack off on her duties at any given chance. Does a woman grow stronger once she's carrying a life in her? Or did Sol toughen her up?

"Let's do this." Sol rises from her seat, and everyone follows her out of reflex. Jihyun pays the bill, and I sluggishly climb the stairs to follow them.

Spare Tire

The sunset spreads across the sky to the west like watercolor. The whites of Sol's eyes glow red like the sun. The free parking lot we are walking to feels like it's a million miles away. The ocean wind is freezing cold. I take back my earlier "The wind is rising, we must try to live!" thing. Who says I have to be consistent with any thoughts I had this morning to last through the night? My eyes well up at the blasts of cold wind. The magnolia flower buds break off their branches as if they're being decapitated.

"Brrr, quick, turn the heater on. What's wrong with this weather? Winter is supposed to be over!"

"Well, there's a saying, isn't there? The spring chill of March kills the unsuspecting elders." Jihyun often comes up with aphorisms that seem too perfect for the situation and it kinda gets on my nerves. I'm glad I'm sitting with my friends in the back seat this time. Sitting by Sol makes me feel calmer. The relentless crashing waves of my heart are quieting down.

After driving for about ten minutes in silence Jihyun says, "I think there is something wrong with the car. Sorry, hold on." He pulls over to the shoulder, opens the hood of the car and looks in, but doesn't seem to find anything. He looks all around the car then kicks a tire, making a *thunk thunk* sound.

He shakes his head. "I think we have a flat."

"Don't you have a spare?" Sol asks.

"There is one, but I've never replaced my tire before. There has to be a mechanic's shop nearby. Perhaps we can replace the tire and ask about the address there."

"If you don't mind, I can take care of it. I've replaced tires before," Sol says.

"Really?"

"I've done it several times. I have a driver's license—a Handicapped Driver's license, but I have it regardless—and I drive trucks and tractors."

Eunyong and I get out of the car and squat by the tire to watch Sol and Jihyun change it, like its entertainment. They take out the spare tire and the tools from the trunk, neatly laying out the wrench and a few other tools I don't know the names of. They lean the spare tire against the flat. Sol places the jack under the joint under the car and carefully lifts the car with the jack. Jihyun helps her pull out the flat tire. Sol in a familiar manner puts the spare in place and tightens the nuts.

I reach out and take Sol's hand covered in grease. "Sol. I don't want to go to the address."

"That's fine," Sol replies nonchalantly, unsurprised.

"Why not?!" I turn to see Eunyong glaring at me from behind.

"Just because." Then I call out to Jihyun, "Can you take us back to the university?"

* * *

"Listen, I don't care if this is my mother or not. Even if, by slim chance, she *is* my biological mother . . . I can't get over that she never reached out to me. Not even once. I thought she was dead or living somewhere abroad, but no, she just never tried to reach me. Why should I reach out to her, when she's perfectly happy without me? You know?"

"There must be a reason, maybe a difficult reason behind that decision," Jihyun carefully speaks up.

I press on. "Please don't interrupt me," I say and return to explaining myself to Sol and Eunyong. "I'm going to stay at Jihyun's place tonight. Please don't take that the wrong way. I just don't have anywhere to go right now. Can you imagine me going back to the room at the café after all that? Or me crashing in Sol's tiny dorm room? No way. I plan to see my dad tomorrow. I'm going to get him to tell me what happened with my mom, who I am to him. I've been avoiding all these questions for a long time, but not anymore. I'm going to see him, get the answers, and then announce my independence from him."

"Don't worry, no one will or can stop you." Sol holds me and dishevels my hair with her dirty hand.

"You are one stubborn girl, Yeoul! You're so close to where your mom is, and you're not going go see her?" Eunyong speaks up.

"She's the one who abandoned me. I'm going to wait until *she* seeks *me*. That might take a thousand years, but I'm still going to wait."

Other than occasionally looking over his shoulder to

the back seat where we sit, Jihyun drives in silence. There is no music playing in the car. The evening street starts to light up. The Youngdo Bridge is not beautiful. Will I be crossing this bridge again someday? Will I find my mother if I climb down to search under this bridge?

"Yeoul. You unlucky, wretched girl. Stop crying. I found you as a crying newborn under the Youngdo Bridge. I decided to adopt you, because you looked so sad. You were swaddled like an abandoned package. But if you keep on crying like that, I'm going to take you right back to the bridge and leave you there just how I found you."
My grandmother told me that story when I begged to leave the late-night town party so we could go home. She hit me in the head with her knuckles. Her breath stank, and her teeth were covered in pepper powder and chives. She told me the same story the evening she didn't feed me. She was busy getting drunk on rice wine. She also told me there's no point in going to school. A pathetic alcoholic, a shriveled-up crone. The worst liar in the world was Grandma.

I notice Sol is sound asleep, leaning on my shoulder. She is like a small bird. Thank you for flying to me. I hold her hand with both of mine. Her hand is rough, small, and bony. For some reason I tear up. *You keep me going, Sol. Like that spare tire, I was tucked away and forgotten in a dark corner for the longest time. I've been an understudy in waiting, never the lead actor of my own life. That's going to change. Now I'm going to do whatever I like. I will keep going. I need you close when I waste away. Don't you dare die before me. If you die, I'm gonna kill you!* Sol turns her head as my shoulder trembles from sobbing.

"Mmm . . . yum." Sounds like she's eating in her dreams. Maybe she's eating one of her mother's apples—the most delicious apples I've ever had—after rubbing it clean against her pants.

Bruschetta con Formaggio e Miele & a Lollipop

In Jihyun's home, a long antique sofa stands on the carpet in the living room. It feels cozy. There's a tree in the corner of the living room, the same kind as the one in the vestibule (lush and green), potted in a ceramic pot.

"It doesn't ask for much care. As long as you water it regularly and keep it in the sun it's happy. My mom thinks they help purify the air." Jihyun nervously puts on his slippers only to take them off.

"Who waters it?" I ask, reaching for the tree. When my hand touches it, several leaves fall off, making rustling sounds. "What was that noise? Do you have a cat?"

"Huh? I didn't hear anything. We can't have pets in this apartment complex. Before my family moved here we had a Yorkshire terrier, a poodle, and a cat. We even had a hedgehog, haha. My father is a real animal lover."

"I had a cat. Her name was Leche. Leche liked drinking, well, leche. Isn't that cute? She was limber, adorable, and extremely possessive. I like to think she is doing well without me."

What are we even talking about? What is this? I suddenly feel depressed, so I walk around and explore the space instead. *Why am I here?* Nobody told me to come here, I walked in with my own two feet, so why am I having these thoughts? I knock my head with my knuckles.

The living room looks like a gallery. Several pictures of his family are hanging on the wall. You can see the chronological progression through the series of pictures: the more Jihyun ages, the more closely he resembles his father. It looks like he will end up bald.

In the first picture, Jihyun is younger than ten. He looks as though he just popped a cherry candy into his mouth. His lips are red, his cheeks are plump, and his eyes are glowing in sweet ecstasy. In the next picture his eyes look the same— large and pretty with his creaseless eyelids—but his facial structure has elongated. His skin tone is so light to the point that he looks translucent.

Looking at these pictures I start wondering: how does a person show improvement with age? People say one matures with time, but how does it manifest? Does the energy in one's eyes change? Does one grow more considerate toward others? Does one show more humility? More self-control? Become more patriotic? As I age, will I become more patient and cultivate a loving attitude toward others? Will I become selfless? Will that really happen just because of age? I remember the day my high school principal retired. It was a particularly hot day and the sun was blazing. During the retirement ceremony the students were told to stand in an open field with no shade, while the principal, and only the principal, got an awning over his head. He went on and on about his accomplishments. People like to say that teaching is a selfless and noble vocation, but he seemed pretty self-absorbed, oblivious to the students' wish for his speech to end so we could clap a bit and head back into the classroom. I don't even remember that oblivious asshole's name. What does it mean to become a "grown-up?" How does one go about doing that, growing up? Will I just become like my parents? I'd like to know if I can actually become a better person. Will I survive long enough to look back at my life and reflect on it fondly?

The last picture, hung closest to the kitchen, is from Jihyun's high school graduation. He is surrounded by a crowd and looks sullen and unhappy with a bouquet of flowers in his arms. It's as though he doesn't want to graduate. His parents are standing on either side of him, forcing a painfully awkward smile. It's in this picture I start noticing his familiar melancholy look. Is this when his parents started talking about separating?

"Stop examining the pictures so closely. You're making me feel self-conscious."

"Whatever, you look so cute in all these pictures."

"Try this." Jihyun, scratching his head, passes a white plate with a toast topped with melted cheese, marbled white and yellow.

I bite into it and exclaim: "This is so good! So warm and moist . . . I think I smell acacia flower honey? What's in it?" I grab the toast with both hands and messily devour it.

"Slow down, there's more. It's called bruschetta con formaggio e miele. You have to use good cheese and honey to make it right. My dad sent me a postcard with the recipe. He likes making this."

"He sounds like a sweet guy."

"He is. A gentle and kind man. So I have a hard time understanding my mother's choice. If she didn't have the affair, we'd still be a happy family."

"Do you hate your mom for that?"

"What? How could I hate my own mother? Without her, I wouldn't exist. I wouldn't have met you. My mom is . . . *different*. She doesn't think like a normal person. It might be because she's a lesbian. No, I don't know. She has too much love to give. She is an open-minded go-getter, intelligent . . . but she's too different from my father." Jihyun pours out his thoughts. He must have been bottling this up. "My dad learned about the affair while he was struggling after his larynx surgery. He couldn't sing professionally anymore. It must've hit him really hard. He made up stories about studying abroad in Italy, and just like that, he left, and I . . ." Tears well up in Jihyun's eyes. He shakes his head. "Sorry. I'm boring you with my sob story."

"No, you aren't." I reach across the table and gently touch the back of his hand. "Your hands are so soft, softer than mine."

"It's your turn, Yeoul. Tell me about yourself. Your parents, your brother, your childhood."

"You know some of it. I told you some when you were visiting me at the hospital."

"Yeah . . . wait, we are using the honorific again. Okay, let's make some rules so we won't keep reverting back to it. There will be a penalty for using the honorific."

"A penalty?"

"You have to grant the other his or her wish."

"Okay. Starting . . . now!" A long silence follows. I smile

a bit, and get up to explore his house, checking out one room and then the other, and then go into the bathroom. The wall and the floor are covered in spotless white tiles. I don't see a single strand of hair on the floor. He must have a maid who comes every day. In this mirror I look vibrant and rosy-cheeked. I wash my hands and turn around to get out of the bathroom, but stop myself to rinse my mouth first. I sit down on the sofa, and the cuckoo bird jumps out of the clock to chirp eleven times. Jihyun breaks the silence.

"You must be tired," he says and laughs. For some reason Jihyun keeps bursting out laughing. What's so funny? He pauses, puts on a straight face, and tries speaking in a serious tone: "Yeoul, you must be exhausted. Going on a road trip right after being discharged was too much."

"Nah, I had fun. Jihyun, how much older are you? Do you really like me dropping the honorific tone when we talk?"

"Yes. I love it. And to answer your question: I'm ten years older than you."

"*Yeh?* What? Ten years?!"

"Penalty!" Jihyun exclaims.

"Huh?"

"You just used the honorific!"

"That was out of reflex. I was startled because I thought you were nine years older than me. You said so before. How old are you again?"

"I'm thirty this year."

"I'm twenty-one. So you are nine years older than me. Why did you lie earlier?"

He giggles. "I wanted to scare you into blurting

something out in the honorific tone. Now you must face the penalty."

"That's cheating. That doesn't count. We have to start over. Okay, no honorific tone, starting . . . now!"

"I didn't cheat, and that totally counts. Remember you have to grant me one wish?"

I don't respond.

"My wish is . . ."

"If it's anything tricky, I'm not gonna do it."

"My wish is for reunification of the Korean Peninsula!⁹ Just kidding. I just want a kiss."

"That's it? Alright, you can't change your mind about it. Come over here." Jihyun scoots over, and I lean in to kiss him. I feel his pulse speed up, but I don't feel anything myself. Why don't I feel excited? Is it because this kiss was imposed on me as a "penalty?" He wraps his arms around me, his hands on my back, and pulls me down to lie on top of his body. I kiss him from above, and his tongue slides onto mine. I taste the honey and cheese from earlier. I rise from his body.

"Are you feeling tired?"

"Yes."

"Okay. You can take a bath. I'll fill the tub for you." Jihyun gets up from the sofa and staggers to the bathroom. I hear the sound of running water. He emerges back out.

"Jihyun, are you feeling alright? You seem a little off."

"No, just nervous."

---

9. "My wish is for reunification of the Korean Peninsula" is a patriotic slogan often taught in Korean schools.

"What are you nervous about?"

"We are going to be sleeping side by side. When I open my eyes in the morning, you'll be right there. It feels like a dream. Don't you feel nervous?"

"Not really. Your place is cozy and nice. Much better than the hospital room."

"Huh. How could you not be nervous to be alone with a man?"

"Dunno. I surprise myself like that."

"Have you . . . slept with a man before?"

"Why?"

"Just answer me."

"What about you?"

"I'm a virgin, a bachelor and a virgin."

"You seem proud of that. Are you one of those people who thinks premarital virginity is everything? Some girls I know told me their lives were ruined when they lost their virginity, their 'innocence.' Innocence is a funny idea to attach to the concept of virginity. How does that work exactly? What, when a hymen breaks, so does her 'innocence?' When a woman gets raped, people act like she becomes some sort of scarlet-letter-carrying sinner, as if she deserves to die. If something like that happens to me I'm not gonna kill myself to make other people more comfortable.[10] I'm going to hunt down the rapist, and get him punished through due process. It's not the woman's

_____

10. There is a tradition in old Korean society in which a maiden would carry a silver knife to kill herself if she ended up in a situation where she could be sexually assaulted.

fault that someone sexually assaulted her. Rape isn't, and shouldn't be, only talked about in a hushed tone. This isn't the same thing, but still, I see a similar pattern even when it comes to lovers. Why is it that it's okay to talk about cuddling and kissing, but once sex is involved everybody has to act secretive? Do I have to act coy, act like I'm a virgin, until I get married? Do you have to? I don't know. As long as one can take responsibility for one's actions, why should anyone . . . I just don't know. Lately I feel like I'm in danger wherever I go, like I'm walking through landmines. Did you notice the men loitering by the hospital earlier? I felt like they were looking at me. Sungyun is part of a gang, you know. Rape isn't just something that happens to women you don't know. Something could happen to *me*. Innocence, virginity . . . I just want to get rid of it on my own terms. By *my* choice. I don't want someone to 'take it.'"

I realize I've been rambling, like the school principal on his retirement day. I burn with self-loathing. I suppose we learn from what we hate.

"Yeoul, you don't sound like yourself. What got you so excited? Your voice got louder, and you are so eloquent when you are angry. I haven't seen this side of you. It's almost chilling."

"This is what I've been thinking all day, and everyday while I was at the hospital."

"Forget about Sungyun and what happened that night. Everything is going to be okay. I will protect you. Forget about it, and if you can forgive him, even better. Remember that your friend is pregnant with his child, and he might end up marrying her. You have to be considerate of your friend's life, right? Are you crying?"

When Jihyun pats my shoulders, I break down. It hurts. I'm so fucking hurt. The tears won't stop. This is the first time I bawled like this since Jimin died. The throw pillow I'm holding in my arms gets soaked.

"I understand how you feel. Do you feel better? You'll feel even better if you wash up and go to bed." Jihyun guides me to the bathroom with his arm around my shoulder. He must have put in bubble bath because the tub is filled with bubbles, overflowing onto the floor, making it slippery. The mirror is foggy. We walk barefoot. He checks the water and then approaches me to hold me from behind. He takes off my new denim jacket and the tshirt with the golden skull, he undoes the brassiere. I cover my breasts with my hands.

"I'll stop here. When I feel sad, I take a bath like this. You'll feel better soaking in a nice warm bath." Jihyun turns to head out.

"Join me. The tub is large enough for both of us."

"No."

"Why not?" I whine.

"Just because."

"You're starting to sound like me. Answer me. Why not?"

". . . I'd want to have sex with you if we got naked together. I want to wait till our marriage."

"You want to marry me?"

"Yes, of course, if you'd agree, that is. Didn't you see the basket of roses the other month? I left a note about that. I felt a little hurt that you didn't say anything about it."

"Wait, that basket of roses? There was no name in the card. I thought it was misdelivered!"

"I thought you'd just know it was me."

"Jesus . . . Look at you, mumbling behind my back. You act as though you're afraid of me. Why can't you look at me straight here?" I uncover my breasts and turn around, and Jihyun slams the door behind him. I want to see a naked man in real life. I want to see if male bodies are really as gorgeous as they are in art, like the statue of David. I want to show my body to the person I choose. I want to share the burden of innocence with him. Is he an ascetic? Autistic? Does he despise me for offering myself like this? Ugh, I don't know, maybe he doesn't want me. Nana or Leche wouldn't take a good look either without the imported dry food I fed them. I enter the tub and blow the soap bubbles, breathing in the luxurious floral smell. I dunk my face into the warm water and hold my breath. I love the way the water hugs my body. I lie down and try floating.

The door opens and Jihyun enters with a big bath towel wrapped around his entire body. He tosses something into the tub: it's the plastic goldfish he bought at Taejong Beach. The stupid fish, a little larger and uglier than a goldfish, swims and tickles my breast.

"Yeoul, listen to me. Let's make a promise. We will not have sex tonight. I hope you will be considerate of this pact."

I laugh. "It's like we are doing a gender role swap. So funny. No worries, I think it's better that way, too. I was actually scared of what might happen tonight. Enough of that. Just come on in. I won't even look at you. Look, I closed my eyes."

"When we are done with the bath, you are heading straight to my mom's bedroom—I made the bed for you—and I'm going to sleep in my room with the door locked. Don't even dream of breaking in, okay?"

"Jesus, I'm not going to break into your room! What an assumption! Don't worry."

We have fun tossing balls of bubbles at each other, splashing and sinking into the water to hide from each other. We try to snatch the goldfish from each other. After horse-playing for a little while the part of my leg that was operated on starts aching, so I stop moving. Jihyun asks, "Can I touch your breasts?"

"No."

"Just once."

"Okay. Can I touch you there?"

"No! Well, okay. But be gentle. I don't want the stitch to pop." Jihyun sounds as though he is about to cry.

"What? Are you hurt?"

"No. I just got circumcised."

I laugh.

Jihyun presses his palm against my breast and quickly pulls back. But then he reaches out with his index finger to touch my nipple. His face looks tense. He is trying to keep it together. I carefully reach down between his legs. There it is. It's hard, and about the size of a lollipop.

Stop, Stop

There is no one on the street. Far away I see a street cleaner walking away with a broom in his hand, but other than that, there is no one around this early in the morning. The air is cold. I find myself coughing. Am I coughing because I went to bed without drying my hair? I woke up earlier than usual. Most nights I wake up in the middle of the night, but last night I slept deeply. The pot of herbal tea and the soft light coming through the curtains was comforting.

It didn't take too long to get to the bus station from Jihyun's place. I should've washed my face before leaving, though. My watch is dead, and I have no way of knowing when the first bus of the day will arrive. My father is probably pacing back and forth or sitting with the newspaper open in front of him. He first started to get up early and pace around in the house a few years ago. The last thing he said to me was, "Watch out for cars." I think he was thinking of Hyunwoo, how we lost him. Does he even worry about me? What will my stepmom say when she sees me? I severed contact for five months after I left, and here I am, limping back. I bet she'd be pretty annoyed by that. She might hit me again. Or kick me out. If I were her, I'd kick me out. I used to feel so much resentment and hatred when I thought of her, but today, I feel sympathy toward her as another woman with her struggles.

I decide to walk home and start to cross the multi-laned road. I pass the yellow divider line. There aren't many cars on the road this early but some cars rush through at crazy speeds. Like I'm in a scene in a movie, I close my eyes and limp across the road. After a few steps, I hear loud honking. A taxi driver lowers the window and screams at me. "You crazy bitch! Are you blind? Go crazy all you want, but don't be a nuisance to others!"

I wanted to see proof of what Kim Inja, Jihyun's mother, talked about as a Presence who looks out for me, but—*voilà.* This brush with death didn't make me feel protected. Or maybe there is a protective Presence, since I'm not dead, but if the Presence kept me from being run over, he's a meddling asshole. With eyes open I run, though still limping, across the road. I yell "Echo!" when I reach the bus station on the other side of the street. There is no echo, no response. If I take the bus from here, I will be going farther away from my father's place. A few people gather, and I hop on the first bus that arrives. I look at the route map. If I get off at the Jagalchi open market, I can transfer to go to Youngdo. I walk all the way to the back seat and sit down. I notice a coin stuck between the seats. I struggle to pull it out. Coin, coin, stuck between the seats, who's the dumbest of them all? The ten-won coin doesn't answer. Dear coin, why the fuck am I going to see her now when she isn't even expecting me and doesn't seem to care to see me? This early in the morning, no less! It's not the coin's fault when it rolls in the direction it's dropped. It's my legs that are taking me to Youngdo, not me.

* * *

"Excuse me, is Sinsun San, building 58 somewhere near here?" I ask an old lady passing by. She is holding a worn Bible to her chest so she must be returning from church.

"What?" She asks as if she can't hear at all. How does she expect to hear the voice of God with those ears? I yell into her ear, "Sinsun District?"

"Yes, this is Sinsun," she says.

I didn't even try that hard, but I am right where I should be! I get so happy, I almost tell a lame joke: is it called Sinsun because *sinsun* (wise spirits) live here? (Har har.)

"Thank you, thank you!" I say instead, "Have a great day. I wish you longevity and the longest and healthiest life!" I realize I am waving my hand at her wildly. The weather is a little depressing, rain drops falling in weird, slow intervals. I enter a windy road and start climbing the uphill path. I see the little hole-in-the-wall stew place. A middle-aged lady is hurriedly gathering the *siregi* herbs that she had been drying in the sun. The smell of miso wafts from the door and tickles my hunger. I should eat breakfast and take my meds. I slip inside and ask the man who appears to be the owner (the man is drinking broth with a bottle of soju next to him, while the lady is still busy in the kitchen), "Excuse me, this is Sinsun District, right? Do you know how to get to San, building number 58?"

He yells to his wife, "Honey! Is building 58 up on the hill?"

"Yes!" She yells back from the kitchen.

"You are going all the way up there? This path will come to an end, and you will reach a hilly area with a lot of reeds. Once you go past there, there are a few houses clustered. Are you looking for someone specific?"

"I don't think you'd know her. Her name is Gang Jinae. I think roughly the same age as your wife. Mid-fifties?"

"Not sure . . ."

"Who are you looking for?" The lady pokes her head out from the hole that connects the kitchen and the dining area.

"Gang Jinae. Do you know her?"

"Just by the name? No. But you look familiar. Where are you from?"

"I live in Busan. I just have one of those faces that looks familiar. I should get going." As I try to leave, the man thrusts out an umbrella.

"Take this, but return it later."

"I'm really okay . . . well, thank you." I bow and climb up the narrow path. The road is not well maintained and it only gets worse as I keep climbing, stairs appearing and disappearing. The fence along the way is half-demolished and coal ashes are scattered about. Another fence has well-done graffiti of a field of sunflowers that makes me want to go lie down in it. I stop to catch my breath. I wish I'd brought some cigarettes. I only have three thousand-won bills and a few coins in my pocket. I'm not sure what to do next.

"Is this San building 58?"

"Yup!" The young woman must be busy; she continues her fast stride away from me. I reach out and grab her arm before she runs off. Rain drops fall on her sweater.

"Do you know the person who lives there . . . Gang Jinae?"

"Of course! Assistant Pastor Gang? She lives right by me."

"She's a . . . pastor?"

"Assistant Pastor, but yes. You aren't here to see her for the service?"

I don't respond.

"Shoot, she won't be home right now. She is at the church leading the early morning service. It's the time for early morning prayer."

"Where is the church?"

"Did you see the main street with the fire station? Once you get there, ask somebody. It's the largest church in Youngdo, so someone there should be able to point the way."

She leaves, but I feel like there is something whispering in my ears, and it's not the sound of rain. I feel like I am on a precarious cliff. A pastor? I feel like it might not be my mom. I hope it's not my mom.

* * *

A few people emerge from the building that looks like the church. Most of them are women. Is that her, the person over there with a bright countenance? She isn't that far away but her face flickers in my vision. She is looking at me! I cover my face with the umbrella. Should I have come this way? I turn around. I start running, slipping in the rain. It's hard to breath. One leg tries to run, the other leg begs me to stop, dragging behind me. Stop, stop. My achy leg struggles against getting farther away from her. How do I keep my body from splitting in two? Please speak, my heart! Suddenly a fire truck rushes by blaring a loud siren, and I feel panicked. I jump onto a bus that is about to leave. I find an empty seat and plop down. The bus stops and goes. There is a huge traffic jam.

"What the hell is going on? Is there a fire or something?" someone complains loudly.

"Don't you see the smoke, lady?" the driver growls. A man taps on my arm.

"Lady, move your umbrella a bit, would ya? My pants are getting soaking wet."

"Oh, I'm sorry." I pass the umbrella to the other hand, and he continues.

"You're taking that home?"

"What?"

"You borrowed that umbrella from me." I realize that the man is the same guy who was eating at the hole-in-the-wall soup shop.

"Oh, I forgot!"

An intense fume of alcohol emanates from him. It's still early in the morning. "Did you find the person you were looking for?"

"Well, yes . . . no."

"What kind of answer is that? People ought to give straightforward answers. You were looking for that lady who goes to church all the time, right? She essentially lives in the church prayer ward. She keeps stopping busy people like me to talk about Jesus and giving me some garbage flyer. Some sort of pastor or minister or something."

"Wait, so you knew who I was looking for. Why didn't you tell me earlier?"

"I remembered after you left. Whatever."

I feel intense abhorrence at this situation in which I am sitting next to this drunk asshole. The smell of stale cigarettes and the alcohol stench from his mouth is repugnant. I feel like my brain is about to explode. I'm going to get off at the next station.

"Churches, Buddhist temples, they're all the same. The world is a rotten place. Rotten through and through." The man hacks up phlegm and spits out the window. "Don't you agree?"

"What?"

"I heard the head pastor at that church got caught with married ladies. Not one or two. Several. It's a big-time shit-show over there. Haven't you heard? Even the kids around this town heard about it, tsk tsk."

I sit in silence.

"So what. Did you meet that pastor or whatever? What's your deal with her?" I jump up to my feet and stagger away from him. As I get off the bus he yells after me. "Where are you going? Don't you need the umbrella?"

Part IV

Interview

I stand before the entrance to my mother's house, under its corrugated metal roof. I don't mean to scare her with my visit. What should I say to calm her down if she embraces me and starts crying? I press down on my chest to calm my pounding heart. With a finger I tuck my wet hair behind my ear. I stomp my feet to shake the dirt and briquette ashes from my shoes. What if she faints?

Knock knock knock. All I did was knock lightly on the door, but the frosted glass rattles like it's going to fall out of the aluminum frame. A dark gray shadow approaches the glass from the other side.

"Who's there?"

"Hi, this is Jeong Yeoul." At my response the shadow freezes, and I can hear her sharp gasp through the door. I feel myself sink into the gloom like when I visited my grandmother's tomb on a gorgeous spring day. Should I have brought a bouquet of flowers here, too?

She opens the door and begins immediately: "Yeoul, welcome. So good to see you. You've grown so much. So tall. I almost didn't recognize you. How have you been?" The greetings roll out of her so naturally it sounds unnatural. She sounds like an old actress auditioning for the lines that she's rehearsed a million times before. The dimples on her cheeks get deeper as she closes the door behind us. I can't tell if she's smiling or grimacing. Why didn't I inherit those pretty dimples? At once I recognize this woman to be my mother. It's not that there are obviously similar features we share. Her face looks like my face in twenty years, pale, slightly tense. I've never seen a pair of eyes that glow so much. She is wearing a long black skirt, a pair of slippers on her feet. Her hand holds a rice paddle. I recognize her blue rubber slippers to be from my dad's factory. The backs of them are torn.

I finally bring myself to open my mouth. "Pastor Gang Jinae? Real name Gang Jongok. You are my mother, correct?"

"Must you talk like that? You must've done some research about me. Come over here, sit down." On the table, there is a small sauce dish of chili soy paste, a few pieces of kimchi, some raw carrot, cucumber, daikon, and some greens. Is she an overly health-conscious vegetarian or something? She places a spoon, a pair of chopsticks, and a bowl of rice in front of me. I think I visibly frowned at the sight of the beans, barley, sorghum, and a few more grains mixed into the rice. I hate that stuff.

"You haven't eaten yet, have you? Let us pray and eat. Father Almighty, thank you. Thank you for leading our beloved Yeoul here, allowing this miraculous reunion." As she drones on with her lengthy prayer, I open my eyes to look at my mother. Her even forehead, her closed eyes, her trembling thick eyelashes. Her pale lips. Her neck, so thin it looks like it will break where it meets her white sweater. Her flat chest. Her bony hands, pressed together, fingers interlaced. Her short hair looks like she cuts it herself. The only furnishing in the house is a futon and a tiny dresser. There is a mirror about the size of a book on the wall. The room feels like it exists separate from the rest of the world. A few tiny pencils, worn down to small nubs. A red ballpoint pen. A Bible and a few books. A few notebooks. The room is so clean and humble that it looks like a prison cell. Is this what she left me for? So she could live like *this*?

"Not sure you'll like what I have, but let's eat."

"Thank you for the meal."

My mother wipes her eyes with a folded tissue, and then unfolds it to place it to the side. It looks like she is thinking of reusing it after the tears dry off. Neatly placed tangerine peels are drying on a chipped plate. A pile of tissue papers. I take off my coat, wet with rain. I look around to see if there is anywhere I should hang it, but no luck, so I put it back on.

"Did you recognize me right away?"

"How could you even ask me that. Of course, you look exactly the same as when you were little. Well, your skin was lighter when you were younger. And I see you everyday with the help of the Holy Ghost. I pray for you first thing in the morning every day. Never, not for a moment, have I forgotten you."

"If that's true, how come you never came to see me? Never a phone call, not even once."

"I've actually gone to see you multiple times. I really wanted to see you. You just didn't recognize me. I used to hang around near you and your granny's house for a while, and by the gate of your middle school, and then your high school. But then I decided that I shouldn't do that. My worry was that you, a sensitive girl, could get upset at the sight of me or become rebellious. What if that sent you down the wrong path? I decided that I'd wait until you become an adult who could understand my choices. The only thing I could do was to pray for you. If it wasn't for our Savior, I would've gone crazy long ago. Or killed myself. I hope you accept Jesus Christ as your Lord and Savior, too."

I forcefully shovel the rice into my mouth, spoonful after spoonful, until it's all gone. She pulls out some gummies and mints from a first aid kit. They're the kind that restaurants keep by the cashier. Mother unwraps a mint and places it on my tongue. I'm no longer a child who'd ask for candies, Mother.

"Did you skip the lecture today? You're majoring in German, right? How is it? Do you like it? You must be reading Herman Hesse, Goethe, all those German masters. But you know, the Bible is much more interesting than novels. There's a reason the Bible has been a best seller throughout the centuries."

"Okay . . ." It sounds like she's the one who did the research. Did she hire someone to tail me or something? Nah, she wouldn't have put in that much effort. I briefly consider telling her that I met Dr. Kim, her friend, that I watched her by the church before running away, that I got off the bus to reluctantly walk to get here, but then I decided against it. There is clearly no point in trying to explain how sad each day of my adolescence was without her.

"Why didn't you remarry?"

"What, do you wish that I had remarried a rich man, so I could give you some pocket money?"

"What?"

"I haven't been with anyone other than your father. I'm married to God."

"Ha," I laugh awkwardly. "Very funny. Why don't you put on any makeup? If you put on some makeup and dye your hair black again, you'd look very nice. Younger."

"I don't care for such things. I like keeping things natural. My silvered hair will turn black soon, anyway. I've been praying for that, so I shall receive it."

Amazing Grace

Mother calmly places her hand over mine. Her hand is cold and rough. Beneath her large pupils, tears well up. I imagine those tears to be cold as the winter rain.

Mother says when I get married and have kids, I will understand. She adds that the easiest way for me to understand her would be sharing her belief in Jesus Christ, but, "That'd be too hard, hmm?"

Like a condescending reporter interviewing a fanatic in a cult, without making eye contact, I spit a few curt questions at her. Her responses are lengthy and complicated each time.

She explains her absence like this: when my father quit his job, which was a fine job, and opened a factory, she had to work herself to death, cooking for all the factory workers while working as well. He slept with almost every female worker and was drinking all the time. One day he brought a woman with a three-year-old son to the house and insisted that they move in. When they started unpacking their things, she had no choice but to leave.

"Why did you abandon me?"

"Well, you are an extension of your father." And she's rambling again. Does she ramble this way because she is a pastor? "Your father's line is tainted. They are all immoral and unethical people. When I looked into the family history, your paternal great-grandfather, grandfather, uncles, they all turned out to have had multiple mistresses and concubines. That blood is in you, and I wanted to sever all connection with your father. I didn't even take his dirty alimony." *Yes, your hands are clean, I get it.* I'm getting sleepy and nod half-heartedly and chime in here and there. Instead of laying out this convoluted story, I wish she'd just reach out and hold me.

My mother proudly shares the story of her bountiful and blessed new life, going to the seminary college as a non-traditional older student, becoming a youth pastor at the church, oh how miraculous it is to be alive, how blessed she is to be able to help other impoverished seminary students. She tells me that I have the blessing of being healthy, I didn't end up a no-good screw-up or a cripple, all thanks to God, as He guarded me as the apple of His eye. *You don't even know me, Mother.* She adds that I need to continue pushing on, living with father, studying hard. I must endure it all until I can move out.

"But, don't you regret anything? Shouldn't you tell me, at least, you're sorry to have left me? I feel like you are rationalizing your choices by using God."

"Yeoul, I didn't have a choice. Don't you get it? If I didn't leave your father, I would've gone mad or killed myself . . . You still don't get it? I see. You are just like him and his sister. You refuse to listen, insist on your point, and you even smile like them, that slimy smile. You are just like everyone else in his family, uneducated and badly mannered, barging into my place unannounced like this! Perhaps we should talk some other time. We can't communicate because we've lived away from each other for too long. You need to leave now. I'm busy today. I need to do the church members' house visits. Thank you for coming. Watch your step on the way down the hill. It's steep." To me, she is acting like an interviewee whose feelings are hurt by my questions.

"Okay, I'll leave. Should I come back to see you some other time, or should I say my goodbyes?"

"Yeoul. Why do you talk like that? Such a tone! Well, considering the culture of the household you were raised in, I understand. Your father's financial situation is probably better than mine, so you should stay with him. Be nice to him. He is a slave to his desires, that poor man. Don't mention seeing me, he might not like that and lash out at you. I hope you do come back to see me, but after you accept Jesus Christ as your personal Lord and Savior. I hope that day comes soon. Goodbye."

As I open the door and walk through it, I hear her immediately start singing behind me. It's as though she's been dying for this inconvenient intruder who ruined her holy morning to leave.

Amazing Grace, how sweet the sound.
That saved a wretch like me.
I regained my lost life, and received the light
Blessed by Amazing Grace.
You lift me up from the swamp of Sin
I thank Thee.

. . .

Over there in Eternity
Basking in the Sun of Amazing Grace
Bright as the Sun we shall sing.[11]

Oh, *so amazing*, I'm sure. Oh, *so blessed*. I lean against the wall to listen to her sing. Amazing Grace. She sings better than Jo Sumi,[12] but Jo's singing style is too contrived. For the life of me I can't sing (I'm always out of tune), but my mother is a great singer. Further proof I inherited my lecherous father's blood, not my noble mother's. No wonder I didn't inherit her dimples.

I pray to God to keep my emotions still. I want to be able to control my tears, this hurt—what did I do to deserve this? Fuck. I should've memorized the Lord's Prayer or something. *Our Father who art in heaven,* please let my feet move. O, I thank Thee, my shoes are moving me. O, dear God. Fuck you, my mother's so-called God! Whether You art in heaven or on this earth doesn't really matter. Father, you motherfucker, you made my life to be your plaything. Did you steal my mother from me, too? Did you command her to sing? Did you damn her to sing for all eternity? Is that her sacred mission that she serves now? Was it you who turned her into a wind-up doll that has to sing or go mad and kill herself? You narcissist motherfucker! Did you turn her into this nauseatingly composed human being? So suspicious and cold to her own daughter? What torture devices

---

11. Koreans have imported this well-known hymn and transformed its lyrics. Translated here is the Koreanized version of the song.
12. Jo Sumi is a Korean celebrity opera singer.

did you use to train her to become the kind of person who doesn't even cry upon seeing the daughter she abandoned at three? You cruel motherfucker! Fuck, did I screw up coming here? Did I do this all wrong? Is this my fault?

Do I even love her? Do I hate her? Maybe it's all the same? Hear me out, o Lord! Didn't you see me whining like a dog, trying to sniff out whether I could stay with her or not? You also saw me chastising her, cornering her with my questions, sneering at her answers . . . God, if you are there, please, call my mother to run out after me, bare feet and all, please hurry, have her yell, "Don't go, Yeoul! Stay. You can live with me from now on. It's never too late to start again, right?" Please make her beg on her knees. Fuck, amen, amen, amen.

I gave God ten minutes but he didn't do anything. God, that lazy piece of shit who doesn't even exist. My chest is caving in. I want to pull out my heart and feed it to the birds and dogs. Peck away, birds, gobble it up, dogs. A cloud of dust floats along at the skirt of the hill. An old man is bending over, and it looks like he is burning something. Ashes fly in the wind. Like crows in formation, the ashes circle around and around. My mind spins with the ashes and becomes infinite.

Algorithm

I feel a twinge of pain in my injured leg. My stomach is upset, too. I feel like throwing up. With the amount of coins I have I can't take the bus and the subway like I did to get here. I have to walk to Gwangbok-dong, and then take the subway from there. I'll go back to Dad, and I will tell him what rights I have to live in his house. To avoid him and his wife is to be defeated. They won't kill me as long as I play along, suck up to them. No shame, no pride. In the definitive pivotal moment I will take a stab, attack strategically. Did my mother's prayer give me the power of wisdom? The word wisdom stinks of slyness and compromise. The moment I started calling the stepmother "Mom," I learned my capacity for wisdom.

There's a cat stretched out in the intersection. I startle and jump aside to avoid stepping on it, but then realize that it's just a fur hat that looks like it came from a Persian cat. It was probably white or cream-colored, but now it looks ashy and ugly from the rain and pedestrians' feet. I squat down to confirm that it really isn't a cat, but a hat. It doesn't look like a fur hat. It looks like a dead dog. A scarf. What the hell is this? Everything in this world is a mess.

•

"What are you doing Yeoul?"

"Oh, hi, teacher! How are you? Do you live in this area?"

"Yeah. I moved here a while back. Do you live here too?"

"No. I just . . . have business to take care of."

"This early in the morning? What kind of business?"

"You know . . . stuff."

"Ha, okay. What are you looking at so intently?"

"Is this really a hat?"

"Ha!" He laughs. "Of course it's a hat. Does this look like a shoe? You still are an oddball."

"Did I seem like an oddball missing a screw back then?"

"Yeah, I guess. That's your charm."

I stay quiet.

"Do you still paint? Speaking of hats, that reminds me: Have you seen the Max Ernst painting *The Hat Makes the Man*?"

"Of course, you put that up on the wall of the art studio at the school. Twenty or so hats forming a shape of man. It was a low-quality print."

"I don't remember putting that up."

"Well, you did."

"Well, let's stop standing around like this, let's get tea. Do you have time right now?"

"A little bit."

The teacher walks ahead of me and I see that the heels of his shoes are worn. His jeans are wrinkled. If he takes off his black jacket, there will be suspenders. He keeps pulling up a shoulder bag strap that keeps sliding off his slumped shoulders. The bag is stained with a speck of blue oil paint.

We arrive at Jasmine, the coffeeshop at the Gwangbok intersection. The shop must have just opened, and the server reluctantly gets up and welcomes us. He takes us to the sofa next to a dying tree. It looks like it might've dried or frozen.

"This tree is a jasmine tree."

"Oh yeah?" I follow with question: "Teacher, how's school?"

"I quit."

"When?"

"The semester after you guys graduated. It's been less than a year but it feels like forever ago."

"Why did you quit? Teaching is a stable job."

"Well, after ten years or so of doing the same thing, it was becoming stagnant. I had no time to make my own art."

Gwangho Lee, my teacher, is a fairly well-known up-and-coming artist. I heard he even got a sculpture into an international biennial art festival somewhere, but, weirdly, here in Busan, not many have heard of him. They say even Jesus wasn't a prophet in his own hometown.

But now I'm remembering hearing a rumor about him being fired for being inappropriate with a girl in his painting class. Was it Hyunmi who told me that? I don't feel like asking him about it, it would be a cruel thing to do. As the person I knew, he wouldn't do things like that. He also didn't have a great relationship with his coworkers, so who knows what happened.

There's a reason why I think highly of him. It was

sometime around June, the last stretch of the monsoon season, in my freshman year. Every school has problems, but our school was rife with bullying. The cliques divided severely. The male and female students were segregated in our school, but the student body was a mix of the rich students from the newly built luxury apartment district and the pre-existing open-market merchants' children.

One fateful day I was late for school, so I ran into the building with my skirt fluttering behind me. Entering the classroom, I let out the sigh of relief because I didn't see any hall monitors or student-conduct-enforcement teachers. But the vibe was weird. Everybody was pacing in and out of the classroom, whispering about something.

"What's going on?"

"Well . . ." The girl who sat next to me was a well-connected delinquent social butterfly. She said Jo Yonguk, a freshman, killed himself by jumping from an apartment building, and the story was appalling. His classmates liked to bully the introverted Yonguk, ostracizing him from the rest of the class, physically bullying him, until one day they said they would stop bullying him if he performed a task they ordered: shoplifting three bottles of imported liquor from the megamart Yonguk's mother worked at. Yonguk was caught stealing those bottles and his mother got fired. That night, Yonguk's sister blamed him and mocked him for the situation. In response, Yonguk stabbed her multiple times with a kitchen knife and proceeded to throw himself off from the top of the apartment building. The school tried to keep it hush-hush and let the whole thing blow over. But my art teacher, Gwangho Lee, made it his personal mission to call out the bullies and to put them through due process. All the students watched from the classroom windows, nearly spilling out, as the parents of those bullies—a businessman with connections to a school board member and a school commissioner were among them—came to get their bratty children. There was a rumor about the art teacher being the only person who touched Yonguk's dead body. We all knew that two of the bullies who were expelled moved on to another school just fine, but we decided not to tell the art teacher.

My homeroom teacher, on the other hand, lectured us to feed our feelings of curiosity and camaraderie to the dogs. Just study silently, we were told, because people who don't go to college are "pieces of garbage." Over time I started to sleep during class, face down on the desk, as though I had made up my mind to become that garbage, rotting and discarded. If I got tired of sleeping, I'd play *Galaga* on my friend's portable video game player. When I got kicked out of class and was made to kneel in the hallway with my hands up as punishment, I considered going out at night to hang out with the boys like my friend suggested, but decided against it. My stepmom would've liked, even cheered me on, seeing me turn into one of those lost-cause girls, on the path to becoming my lowest self. I never even missed a single class. Instead, I went to the art room after school. I'd paint grotesque shit. The art teacher once caught me stabbing my sketchbook with a pencil knife.

On the other hand, my brother, Hyunwoo, really got into being a good student around the time Yonguk died. They'd been in the same class, and Hyunwoo studied like he'd die if he didn't. The math genius that everybody complimented was born around this time. Calculus, confusing graphs, 3-D vectors filled his notebooks. One day I went to his room because I wanted to listen to his Velvet Underground tapes, but he gave the entire box to me.

"They are yours now."

"What?"

"I'm not going to listen to music anymore."

"Why?"

"I'm tired of things that can't be proved."

"What are you talking about?"

"I'm tired of music and its unsolvable problems." He walked out of the room holding a glass of water, and that was it. There was a thick book open on his desk.

"Please leave. I don't want to see you."

From then on, Hyunwoo stopped listening to music altogether, not even radio at night. He also acted like he couldn't see me. He stopped peeking through the bathroom door while I bathed, didn't ask through the door if I was constipated, and he didn't blush when I stared at him. He stopped telling me, "Stop talking back at Mom," or, "You have no talent for painting. Give it up and prepare for college." He didn't even say it half-heartedly.

* * *

"Yeoul, do you still paint?"

"Nope, I quit."

"Quit? You make it sound like painting is the same thing as drinking or smoking. Don't think about life in terms of closed-off segments, marked with quitting. Continue flowing with it."

"Says you who quit teaching. What are you up to lately?" Without even thinking about it, I grab a cigarette out of his pack and light it. For a moment he stares at me, then he follows my lead and lights a cigarette for himself. We look at each other in silence, then laugh.

"I opened an art studio to teach classes. Gotta pay the bills." He hands me the card. "When you have time, come in and teach the kids, will you? I need to work on my upcoming exhibition."

"Maybe. I'll have to see."

"Okay. How's Hyunwoo. Do you guys still butt heads like before?"

"No."

"I remembering him being on the top of the class, very smart. Didn't he go to KAIST?"[13]

"No, he got accepted into Seoul University's physics department. And he went."

"Is that right?"

"My parents didn't have enough money to support both of us. If I hadn't gone to college, Hyunwoo would've been able to pursue what he wanted. If he hadn't gone to Seoul, that thing wouldn't have happened. So my parents treat me like a thorn in their sides. They think it's my fault that Hyunwoo had to move so far away from us. That might be true. I mean I demanded to be sent to college, you know, *Hyunwoo isn't the only human with rights in this family!* If I had

_____

13. Korea Advanced Institute of Science and Technology.

known college was a bummer like this, I would've just gone to work in the factory."

"What are you talking about? If you could both go to college, that is of course the ideal arrangement. It's another story if you failed the college entrance exam. And Seoul isn't that much farther away from Daejeon." He let my silence linger for a moment. "Did something happen to you guys?"

The teacher doesn't usually pay close attention to others, but once something captures his attention, he digs in. Nothing good comes of it but he does it, like that June my freshman year. I guess artists need to get themselves overinvolved.

"No, nothing. I'm rambling like I've been drinking! Sorry about that."

I borrowed a ten-thousand-won bill from him with the promise that I would soon come by the studio to teach a class. I get the feeling that I won't be able to deliver on the promise. My eyeballs feel like they are going to fall out. I woke up too early this morning. Today feels like it's taking a million years to pass. When I return to being alone after meeting someone, I regret everything I said and feel deep in my bones how trivial life is. I might be a speck of paint or ink that was accidentally rubbed off on someone. My soul is evaporating.

Russian Blue

There is a ladder. It's made of wood, its rungs are narrow, and it leans against the wall. I believe the ladder has been there since before we moved here. You'd never know it's there, though. Only when the ivy's vines dry out and the leaves fall off does it reveal itself. The ladder only shows itself to those who seek it, always hiding under the ivy, behind the persimmon tree. I buried a glass jar under the ladder. Inside the jar there are photographs, letters, locks of hair, and a little musical ocarina . . . I don't remember what else. So many secrets are filling me up . . . Perhaps I buried the jar because I *didn't* want to remember what I cherished. If possible, I want to cover my memories with vines. I want to be buried like a glass jar under the tangled grass. I'm too tired.

"Leche, I'm home!" Dad looks up in the middle of cutting his toenails, curled up into a ball over the newspaper. In his wide, surprised eyes, I see something that resembles anger. He drops his head and collects the toenails. "Where's Leche?"

"Where have you been? I heard you ran away from home." My aunt, or actually my stepmother's youngest sister who runs a hair salon in Daegu, takes a jab at me.

"What are you doing here?" I ask coldly.

"Look at her," my aunt says to my father as if I'm not here. "You act like I shouldn't be here! Your hair looks terrible. You look like a drowned rat. Take a shower, then I'll give you a haircut."

I sneer. "You are so predictable."

"What's predictable? They say the tamest cat is the first one to jump on the stove. You've been going around town like a cat in heat. *That's* predictable."

"Screw you. Don't make me laugh. Where's my cat? And what are you cooking? That pot is huge. My cat could fit in there. Where is she?"

My father interrupts. "Shut up! You keep popping in and out of the house as you please. Don't act like you live here. And what, as soon as you get back, you don't even say hello to your own parents, too busy looking for your cat?"

I turn to my father. "Well, did *you* say hello to your own daughter? You never treated me like a person. You wish I would die on the street, don't you? You must be so disappointed that I keep turning up alive."

"The way you talk . . ." He grits his teeth.

I hear a purring sound coming from my room and turn away from him. "Leche, is that you? Baby, your sister is here." I walk into my room.

What the hell. Beneath the window where Leche and I liked to look out to the street below, against the wall with the torn wallpaper Leche liked to scratch, a baby is whimpering. The crib is filled with lacey blankets—it looks like it's topped with cream—and a baby sticks her little hand out and waves. My stepmother is spooning powdered milk into a bottle.

At first, my stepmother seems startled at the sight of me walking in. But then she casually taps the measuring spoon against the bottle and drops it into the powdered milk container.

"Yes, yes, little Yeondu. Hungry, aren't you? Let's have some milk." Gently holding the baby like a fragile and precious object, my stepmother stares mockingly into my face. I flinch and step back, closing the door behind me.

"What is that? Dad! Who is that?"

"Lower your voice. You are scaring the baby!"

"Whose baby is that? Where's Leche?"

"Of course he's your brother. I gave away the cat. I heard cats are bad for babies."

"No way. Fuck this. Give me back my baby!"

"A cat isn't a person. Don't call a cat a baby. I gave some cat food and the litter box to the person who adopted her, so Leche will do just fine. If you're worried, go check on her, I won't stop you."

"So you threw out my baby, and adopted this baby? Wait, you guys *made* him? You and Stepmom? At your age? Why? When did she get pregnant?"

"You knew that. I told you last summer. You don't care about your family. Where's your mind?"

"Don't lie! Can you even have sex at your age? You're a sex-addicted monster! A slave to your own desire! You can't even take care of what you've already ejaculated!"

An awkward and bitter silence hangs in the air.

"Yeoul, you idiot. Stop stressing out your mom. Your mom had a hard time giving birth at forty-five. She had a bad case of pre-eclampsia. Stop being a brat, you're grown up now! Haven't you watched *Extraordinary Stories from Abroad*? People conceive children in their seventies and eighties now. So stop with your psychotic act and take a shower. Eat some seaweed soup." My so-called aunt tries to put a towel against my tear- and snot-covered face.

"Don't touch me! Just go home! Take your sister with you! Why do I need to call her Mom? I have my own mom! That *woman* had a husband and a child before all this, right?" I turn to her. "How could you act like none of that happened and live with another man? Even beasts don't do that. I'm not going to be like you!"

Dad hits me across the face.

"How many times do I need to tell you? Your stepmom is not that kind of person. I don't know where you heard those stories, but we love each other. That's why we stay together. The woman who gave birth to you despised me. What's the point in me saying all this . . . Hyunwoo and you are both precious to me. And that goes the same for the baby in the room."

"Well, keep on loving each other, for thousands and thousands of years."

"Yeoul, sit here. Tell me, what brings you home? You weren't gone for a month or two, no, you were gone for six months! Tell me where you've been."

"Why? Don't you hate that I'm back? What do you want to know? You didn't worry a bit, I don't think. You even changed the lock!"

"When did you stop by? There was a minor burglary, someone took the camera, so your mom changed the lock. We thought you might've taken the camera. We worried you wouldn't come back if you kept making money with petty theft."

"What? Oh, I remember now. You believe all the bull-shit stories that woman tells about me. Forget it. You don't hear anything I say, do you?"

"Honey, honey!" Stepmother walks out into the living room. I'm surprised it took this long for her to jump in. "Honey, don't bother. She's just feeling all uppity because she got to see her mom. That ungrateful bitch. Tell her to leave!"

I drop my head like a soldier who'd lost the will to fight on. I stuff my feet into my wet sneakers, crumpling their backs. There were things I so badly wanted to ask— *Did you worry about me? Did you miss me? Did you worry about my mom? Do you think about her? Would you like to meet her again someday?*—Why didn't I ask these questions before? What was I afraid he'd say? I wanted to tell him that I found her, that now we could all get together. I planned to act all mature, to say it like I was giving advice. Come on, you guys need to see each other at least once before you die, no? How about you guys bury the hatchet before it's too late?

But now I get it. It's all pointless. I get this too: I didn't announce my independence like a Korean fighter against the Japanese colonists, but I am officially emancipated. I don't need to come up with an eloquent Declaration of Independence. I don't need to nudge him. *I hear Americans move out when they graduate from high school. So I will too.* Everything is cleared up. Easy peasy.

No. I believe my dad will soon run out the door to stop me from leaving. It's just taking a while for him to put on his shoes because he's heavy. His eyes will be bloodshot, he will reach out to grab me, keeping me from leaving. I wait in the empty lot in front of my house, kicking around a deflated ball. The flat ball rolls over to the torn vinyl greenhouse. I have no energy to go after it. I'm hungry and my eyes hurt. I decide to believe that my father tried to run out after me, but my stepmother and aunt stopped him, saying things like, *No, this is a good thing. We don't need to pay her tuition any longer. She must be damaged goods by now, anyway. No one would want to marry her. It's better to kick her out now. She needs some hardship to scare her straight.*

Father wholeheartedly trusts whatever my stepmom says, like, "Things were fishy between Yeoul and Hyunwoo, even though they are supposed to be sister and brother. She must've coaxed naive Hyunwoo into changing his major. She must've asked for pocket money from him—why else would he have gotten a part-time tutoring job? That's how he got into a car accident late at night!" If my stepmother said it, my father believed it. Even a lovesick, no, libido-sick fool like my father should be able to see how absurd these accusations are. Someday I will clear things up. There will be a chance for me to tell him everything.

It's raining again, and the cold wind is blowing. Whether it was the camera that was swiped or how I'm swiping my tears, it doesn't matter—it will rain, wind will blow, and once the rain stops, new, green leaves will sprout and spread. Aged trees will still bloom, fruits will grow off the branch and dangle helplessly before they fall. The old trees will bloom and fruit again. Stepmom once told me, *If your father didn't stop me, I would've had five more children with him. It was your fault I had to abort three of my children.* She ripped my books and notebooks into shreds while glaring at me hatefully. I don't think I will ever understand her obsession with having more children, but I can almost see why she hated me. My cat knew when I was ignoring her, and she ripped up the scratching mat with her fierce claws. If I step back and think about it, my stepmom is a sad person. Is God laughing at the sight of my stepmother's aborted babies, bloody and torn? Is he saying, *Come to me. I'm the Way. I shall save you?* How much of a sick bastard is God? How awful can life be that humanity needed to come up with a fantasy like God?

A Game of Roulette

I'm still fuming. I want to beat someone up or be beaten up. I wouldn't hesitate to taunt a world-class boxer. Hello, Mr. Stone Hands, let's see what you've got.

Dark clouds are gathering, and the sky is darkening to the color of Russian blue, like my Leche's eyes.

My home, no, the house that my father, the evil step-mom, and their baby—was his name Yeondu?—live in is on the uphill road that leads into the forest from the Temple Beomuh subway station. To get there from the station you have to walk past the city cemetery and go farther into the forest until you see a small cluster of houses. Taxi drivers are reluctant to drive anyone there because there is nearly no chance of finding a customer on their way out.

When my dad was running a factory workshop at home and my grandmother was dying from lung cancer, I was taken back by my father. I held his hand to his car, got in, and arrived at his place—our home was the largest house in the entire town. It was always loud with machines and workers, but father was rarely stressed out about money. The men at the workshop teased and bullied me, but it wasn't unbearable. I heard the slippers we produced in the work-shop sold very well. My father couldn't produce enough to meet the demand, so he and his friend decided to build another workshop, a huge factory. They got cutting-edge machinery and recruited more workers. Our family moved into a western-style two-story house in Sajikd District. We had a live-in maid and driver. My father drank and partied, and Stepmom didn't have to do any chores. But neither of them gave me any money or bought me the things I needed, like underwear, so I shared underwear with the maid. My crotch was so itchy when I shared underwear with her, and she told me, "I caught the crabs from your dad, anyway."

In less than three years my father's business went bankrupt, and we had to move to the apartment complex when I started the second year of middle school.

People say, "When the rich go bankrupt, they still get their meals for three years." Perhaps that was the case for us, since I don't remember Stepmom or Dad working. They sure demanded that we tighten our belts, though. But I recall seeing my stepmom going shopping, my dad's golf clubs in the car trunk. They kept buying Hyunwoo perfectly fitting pants as he grew up, but would scold me when I outgrew the school gym uniform. It's no good for a girl to grow so tall, you better stop eating so much food, they said. If I talked on the phone with my friend for too long, Stepmom would pull out the cord and throw it against the wall. She grew hysterical every day, and the quarrels between her and my dad grew more frequent.

I've been walking down the road, tracing my memories for quite a while but am still far from the subway station. I stop at the city cemetery bathroom. I need to pee and wash my face. In a rush, I run into the stall, and sit on the toilet.

It feels unhygienic and a little creepy, so my pee comes out in hesitant spurts. What is this strange noise that I hear? Is someone sobbing? No, I don't think that's it. It sounds like Leche's whining. I leave the stall to search for the source of the sound, and knock on the next stall. I don't hear any response. Did I imagine that? Is there a stray cat in here? I drop to my hands and knees and bend down to look under the stall. I see a pair of sneakers, a boot. I knock on the door loudly.

"Is everything okay?"

No response.

When I press my ear against the door I can hear strained breathing.

"Crazy assholes." I mutter to myself and turn around to wash my hands and face. The bathroom door flies open and two people spill out.

"What the fuck did you call us? Crazy assholes?" A girl who looks a lot younger than me, at best a middle schooler, yells at me without using the honorific.

"Yes, that's what I said. What are you going to do about that?"

"So you got a gaping piehole you can't control, huh?" The girl's fist in the air trembles. Her other fist is holding a pair of hot-pink panties. Her boyfriend smirks like he was watching some sort of tournament.

"Your panties are off, I see. What were you doing in there? Making porn? Your mom's blood hasn't even dried from your scalp yet, you baby . . ." As I say this I feel in my gut, *Oh shit, this is a bad idea.* Her fist flies into my face. I fall to the ground, hitting my head against the door. I crawl on my elbow to grab her boot, but her sneakers give my head a good kick. I spin on the floor like a windmill. *I give up, I give up, sorry, sorry!* I'm so scared they will keep kicking me, but they stop at my surrender. Perhaps they are drained from what they were doing in the stall. They tell me to pay up instead. I hand over the eight thousand won, all the money I have, but beg for some change so I can pay the subway fare. They look proud, like they won a prize from spinning the Wheel of Fortune. I actually feel pretty good, too. My chest feels lighter now that my nose is bleeding. I can make more money. And I have a good amount of money in the bag I left at Jihyun's place. Money saved from the café and German tutoring. Jeong Yeoul, you are doing your best. Good job! And these wounds are just mild scratches. Wait, no, they'll probably leave some serious marks. Shit, where did those little assholes go?

Bravo, My Life

"After I come back, she and I will get married." I hear Jihyun saying to Donghyuk, his best friend, as I'm coming out of the bathroom after a shower. I feel like he is saying it for me to hear.

"Is this bastard for real?" his friend asks me.

"Of course." Jihyun doesn't give me a chance to speak, and starts rambling. "Yeoul, you can keep going in college as a married woman. I'm going to persuade my father in Italy. My mom is more or less on board. Don't worry about a thing. You want this too, right? I take that as a yes." Jihyun and Donghyuk seem pretty wasted. When I arrived at Jihyun's place for my bag, there were already several empty wine bottles on the table. Jihyun was surprised to see my mangled face, but Donghyuk acted as though he expected it.

"Sungyun did that, right?" Donghyuk asks. He goes on to tell me my attacker has been looking for me, inquiring about my whereabouts. He paid off the police, too, so that their investigation won't go anywhere.

★ ★ ★

Jihyun lifts the piano cover and starts to play. This man is capable of all kinds of things.

"No, no, no. Play Erik Satie. '*Je te veux*,' I want you." Donghyuk grabs my hand and places it on his shoulder, and wraps his hand around my other hand. His left hand holds my waist. I am held awkwardly against his chest as he leads me in a circle. Continuing with his piano, Jihyun turns to look at us. He smiles.

"This is called a waltz. Yeoul, you're a natural."

"Yeah?"

"You'd learn how to dance quickly, I think." There's a pause and then Donghyuk presses his nose against my cheek to sniff. "Yeoul, you smell very nice."

"You must be smelling the shampoo. I want to stop." I plop down on the carpet, but the piano won't stop. "Jihyun, where is my bag?"

"I hid it."

"Give it back!"

"For what? You didn't seem to have much in there."

"I have to take care of some business."

"It's getting late. Can't it wait?" Donghyuk brings in a new bottle of wine, stabs the cork with the opener. There is cheese and smoked salmon too.

"Yes, Yeoul, don't leave. Let's drink! After tomorrow you won't see Jihyun for a while."

"Jihyun, when are you leaving?"

"The flight is on the day after tomorrow, but I need to leave for Seoul tomorrow. I'm spending the night near the airport so I can catch the early flight. I wish you could come with me, but you don't have a passport, do you?"

"I have no such thing, no."

"While I'm gone, get yourself one. You need one for our honeymoon trip."

"Who said I'd marry you?"

"That nonsense again! We bathed together, and we saw everything. So . . ."

Donghyuk grabs his head with both hands and squeals, "Wait, you guys are at that stage? Yeoul! Are you really going to marry this homo? He can't get hard with women. His cock is tiny, like this!" He lifts his pinky, and Jihyun wraps his arm around Donhyuk's neck, pretending to put him in a choke hold.

"Donghyuk, stop kidding around! Stop making shit up, you drunk asshole!"

"What are you talking about? I shouldn't marry Jihyun?"

"You don't even know him very well. What do you love about him?"

"I think I know him somewhat. He went on several blind dates intended for an arranged marriage, he dated a Miss Korea, he is quite a bit older than me, but . . . he is nice, rich . . . I don't think I can find someone like this again. Did you marry the café owner because you loved her?"

"Well, love is an illusion caused by hormonal confusion."

"I have a contrarian streak, so now I want to marry Jihyun. We're going to have so many babies, enough to start a soccer team. We will live happily ever after till the end. Jihyun, I'll be waiting here, come home as fast as you can, okay? How many days will you be in Italy? You're coming back soon, right?" I kiss Jihyun's forehead. I feel like that's not enough so I kiss his eyelids and lips. I don't know if it's about being caught off guard or Donghyuk being there, but Jihyun pulls back, muttering, *Wait, wait.*

The three of us drink in silence. I don't think I like wine. Donghyuk tells me I'll like it soon enough if I train my palate and continues refilling my long glass with the golden drink. I think I'm not born to be high-brow. Jihyun lies down on the couch. He doesn't seem to feel well. Why wouldn't he go to the bed?

I find my bag, and check if the wallet is still in there. My books and other belongings must be still at Instant Paradise or in the apartment in that building. Oh, but Sol and Eunyong got them for me. They must be still in the trunk. I should grab them in the morning.

"I'm going to step outside for a minute. When Jihyun wakes up, tell him I have his key, so he can lock the door and go to bed. Are you going to stay over tonight?"

"You're taking off in the middle of the party? Lame." Carrying a glass in each hand, Donghyuk stumbles after me to the door. He pushes one of the glasses into my hand and clinks the other one against it.

"Cheers to Yeoul's future! To our brief youth!"

Opening Ceremony

It's been a while since I was on campus. Sol would probably nag me if she saw my face. What happened to your face?
Did you get into another fight? How's your leg? What's this
smell from your coat? What would you like for the evening
snack? She'd ask all these questions at once.

The campus is deserted. At this time last year, mid-
March, when I was a freshman, there were small groups of
students hanging out here and there. A well-dressed couple walk toward me from the clock tower. The girl is holding her books against her chest instead of keeping them in
her backpack.

Today is the longest day of my life. I head to the café
to find Eunyong so we can search for Sol together, but the
café's sign is off. 10:15 is too early for the shop to close. I
think about going into the café, but I have a bad feeling. The
dim light seeping out the door looks like that of a bathhouse, except it feels like these lights aren't dimmed to make
people more comfortable, but to conceal something.

I feel like I can't make sense of anything unless I trace
my turbulent day with Sol. Why am I so weak and indeci-
sive? Eunyong is street-smart and practical, but it looks like I
won't find her tonight. Jihyun and I can communicate only

so far. He's also leaving for Italy the day after tomorrow, so I don't want to burden him with complicated stories. I feel like someone is following me, and I keep turning around to check. Only mindless pedestrians going their way.

I pass through the narrow passage behind the Humanities building to get to the female students' lounge. The acrylic sign dangles. Sol, please be here. I think I might just pass out if you are not here, gone to the dorm or copy room or dining room.

The door opens before I muster the courage to approach it. A woman calmly steps out of the Female Student Association's official meeting room. She bends her knees and starts to lock the door.

"Wait!"

"Huh? Yeoul Sunbe?"

"Is no one in there? Where's Park Sol?"

"I was waiting for you this whole time. Hold on." I follow Yeonju into the room, feeling dumbstruck. Yeonju at first seemed strangely distant and severe, but she proves my first impression wrong. The room is disheveled. She opens the gray cabinet and pulls out something from behind lumps of papers and pens. "Sol Sunbe told me I have to give this letter to you. She told me I *have* to make sure you receive it." Yeonju hands me what looked like a leftover invitation from a past event and takes off her glasses to carefully wipe them.

"What's this? You were waiting for me this whole time for this? Were you covering yourself with this dirty blanket to keep yourself warm? Have you eaten?"

I walk Yeonju to the back gate and wait listlessly. I look

around to see where I should go. I heard there are under-cover cops everywhere on campus. I walk slowly, past the student building, then the old library that just lit up, and the darkened Arts building. The bronze statues seem to be turning their heads and twitching. They're watching me. I keep looking for a better place to be alone.

After passing the granite walls of the museum, the Bridge on the River Kwai appears. It's just a rusty metal bridge, but we call it that. Beneath the bridge is a deep ravine. Sunbes call it the valley Mirinae, like the Milky Way . . . a barred spiral galaxy, billions of planets, black holes, even the deepest darkness become beautiful the moment someone gives them a name. The rocks protrude into the sky and water gurgles as it flows through them. If I had to choose a favorite spot on campus, this would be it. One day when acacia flowers were in full bloom, Sol and I sat on the Bridge on the River Kwai, dangling our legs and singing. To be more precise, I was learning a song called "When the Day Arrives" from her. When both our voices were getting hoarse, I handed her a postcard. I positioned the card in a way that the picture of a mysterious girl flying through the night sky was at the top.

Sol recognized the painting. "Chagall's *Acrobat*." She enunciated the English title, then translated it into Korean: *A Jester*. She had to be a show-off as usual. She told me Chagall painted for the masses. Flowers, trees, forests, people, houses—they all exist in his paintings for the people.

"Nah, that doesn't sound right," I said, but didn't insist on it. I don't remember what I actually wrote on the post-card. I think I closed by saying I really liked her. That we were sisters, bound by friendship thicker than blood. I think

I might've written *Let's not change* but then erased it because I felt embarrassed about it. Also because I felt bad about Jimin Sunbe for some reason. Did I cry a little then? Wait, was it Jimin, not Sol, who sat by my side like a small gift box?

There are a few lit streetlamps by the bridge. One, two, three . . . I take twenty-one steps along the bridge. My age. It's too young for certain things but too old for some other things. With those steps, I end up in the middle of the bridge. When I sit down, the bridge is cold against my butt, but I can take it. I look around. No one is here. I lick my finger to open the folded letter. It feels like a late reply to my postcard. Three pages. My heart is thumping, but there is a lightness upon seeing the letter: *Sol's handwriting is terrible,* I chuckle.

Hey friend,

How was last night? I don't know for certain when you'll receive this letter, but I suspect you received it today. I'm right, aren't I? (Remember, I can foresee everything.) Hehe, did you sleep with him? Jihyun, that old man, he seems like a nice person with lots of money. But he's not really cute, don't you think? Jihyun, that old man, he seems like a nice person with lots of money to whom you should feel grateful for what he's done for you. But he's too pale, don't you think? Okay. Are you going to marry him? If you love him, I guess that shouldn't be a problem, but I was just wondering. Can I offer you some advice?

I ask you to reconsider your decision to be with him, if you are only with him for his support during the difficult times. We need to directly face the confusion, scarcity, and despair. We must endure the present. What I'm trying to say is that the problems don't go away even if you flee under the wings of a supporter, under his shade. (To be entirely honest, I'm blinded by jealousy, so I don't really know what I'm talking about. I know you need security and a sense of peace more than anything, but I'm afraid you will go away somewhere safe, somewhere far away with this man, and I love you.)

More than anything, I question whether I deserve to give this advice, since I'm fleeing myself, going into hiding. Do you know what I'm talking about? You were hospitalized during it, so you might not know the situation in detail, but you might've heard the news coverage. The student occupation at the American Cultural Service building? At the time, a few Sunbes who support North Korea's Juche ideology got arrested, and the Female Student Association's president, Boyong, is wanted by the police. I'm not safe either, apparently. Remember the sign I OPPOSE THE IMPORT OF FOREIGN PRODUCE? The one we hung on the American Cultural Service building during the occupation? I wrote that (in my terrible handwriting, of course) with paint as a member of Patriotic Students Who Oppose Foreign Powers. My name could definitely come up during an interrogation and torture. There are too many political factions on campus, and the college is controlling some of them with the promise of scholarships. It's just not safe to be on campus, that's for certain. I want to love my enemy, but I don't even know their faces. Here's a secret: I have an enemy within me as well. The enemy wants to study without causing trouble, win a scholarship, pass the exams. The enemy howls that she doesn't want to waste the money her mother made by selling apples on the side of the road and her father by embalming. That enemy tries to persuade me that I can help the weak after I get a stable job as a pharmacist. So she limps to the library even in her dreams. She is pathetic. She doesn't care about democracy, freedom, or justice—those are just big ideas to her—and she doesn't care to serve the People. She watches the Sunbes who became career politicians on the basis of their past involvement with student protests. I constantly ask myself if a person can serve others without an ulterior motive, without immoral desires.

Hehe, do you like me writing in this dark, sardonic tone?

By the time you read this letter, I will probably be in hiding. You won't find me crashing at a friend's place or at my parents' house. I'm tiny, so it'll be easy for me to hide. Don't waste your energy, is what I'm trying to say. But don't worry. We will meet again. I want you to know how much I trust you and love you. I'll be back for the May 1st festival like nothing happened. I plan to host a gay and lesbian festival. Of course, neither of us is a real lesbian, but . . . well, what do I know. Are you certain about your sexual orientation? Anyway. I dream of a community that embraces all marginalized minorities—people with various sexual orientations, people with disabilities, the impoverished urban population, sex workers. I hope you also have a dream. There is no such thing as complete despondency.

Don't overthink your problems at home, don't blame yourself for the deaths of others. I think you do those things *either because you are genuinely dumb, or you have some sort of romanticized masochistic tendency. You're a little perverted, but I believe you will become healthier. Don't laugh. Believe me.*

I got to know Eunyong thanks to you. I'm a little torn. There are a lot of dangers swarming around her. Sungyun is a serial rapist and a thug. He may have committed theft or murder too. He seems like a psychopath. Don't get ahead of yourself and put yourself in danger. Be safe.

The sun is rising. I've been here all night. I haven't slept. Whenever I hear someone dragging her shoes as she walks by, I look out, thinking maybe it's you. The Humanities building has been strangely quiet.

A week from now (March 21st, 3 PM), I'll meet you there. You know where—the river we went to that day? You don't seem to get it. Fine. I guess I have to give you a hint: a story with "backbone." I've been speaking in code this whole time. Did you notice? I doubt this writing will fall into the wrong hands, but just in case. I didn't even use your or my real name for that reason. Do you like the tone I'm writing in? You like Nietzsche. I'm trying to imitate Nietzsche's tone, or more accurately, I'm writing in a mode of awkward translation. It's so fun to write like this, isn't it?

Time to close this rambling letter. I'll close with a postscript, a quote from Nietzsche.

I'll wait there. I miss you. Don't rush.

P.S. Whoever will have much to proclaim one day must long remain silent unto himself. Whoever intends to ignite lightning one day must long be a cloud.

Tears pour from my eyes. They've been flowing for a while. What's happening to me? I don't think tears are somehow more sacred than any other excrement like snot, saliva, urine, blood, or pus. No, I'm not thinking anything. Nothing at all. I just cry and laugh. I don't understand everything Sol is saying here, but that doesn't matter. The stars are beautiful tonight. But as I look up at the sky, it's not the stars twinkling I want to understand, it's the darkness that the stars hang against, and the darkness that hangs behind that. The impenetrable darkness that neither lightning or fire can break through, the darkness I can see between the branches where the sky and the land merge. Is there more darkness behind that darkness? I rub my eyes but it's still not clear where I am. I feel like I'm locked in a strange prison called The World. There has to be an Exit. Of course there is.

Okay, I can do it. I have the courage within me. Now I'm ready to start. With my friend, and with slow, steady steps, one after another . . . I rub my face hard with my palms. I make fists with my hands. I like myself right now. The trees exhale fresh air and the water murmurs around me. I want to be kind to those who have been cruel to me. I fold the letter and stand up.

In the distance I see a long, blue shadow approaching. Someone is walking toward the bridge. I lean against the railing so they can pass me. From the other direction, two more people walk toward the bridge. The metal of the bridge rattles. Is it my legs that are rattling or this old metal bridge? Why are there several men in dark suits walking from opposite directions to this bridge at night?

"Get her! Now! Don't let her escape! We'll make sashimi out of her tonight!" It's a familiar voice.

The men rush at me. Oh shit, I find myself hopping onto the railing. Leche is good at landing lightly like this. And I—like the girl in *The Acrobat*—I spread my arms, and cross my left leg in front of the right. I spin my arms in a circle like a propeller, but my body does not fly up into the air. Quite ordinarily and simply, I move.

Kim Yideum is an outspoken feminist hailed as one of the greatest poets in South Korea today, and her works in translation include *Cheer Up, Femme Fatale* (Action Books, 2015), and *Hysteria* (Action Books, 2019). Having received her PhD with a dissertation on Korean feminist poetics, she has taught at Gyeongsang National University, served as a culture columnist, and hosted a poetry radio show. She has received numerous awards for her poetry, including the Poetry and the World Literary Award (2010), the Kim Daljin Changwon Award (2011), the 22nd Century Literary Award (2015), and the Kim Chunsoo Award (2015). Ms. Kim owns and operates Café Yideum, a bookstore–café, in Ilsan, a satellite city of Seoul. *Blood Sisters*, originally published to great renown in South Korea in 2011, is her debut novel.

Jiyoon Lee is a poet and translator whose most recent publications include *Poems of Kim Yideum, Kim Haengsook, and Kim Minjeong: The Collection of Contemporary Korean Poetry* (Vagabond Press, 2017). Her translation of Kim Yideum's book of poetry, *Cheer Up, Femme Fatale* (Action Books, 2015), was shortlisted for the Lucien Stryk Prize. She is also the author of *Foreigner's Folly* (Coconut Books, 2014), *Funsize/Bitesize* (Birds of Lace, 2013), and *IMMA* (Radioactive Moat, 2012). She received her MFA in Creative Writing from the University of Notre Dame.

PARTNERS

pixel ||| texel

<u>ADDITIONAL DONORS</u>, CONT'D

Richard Meyer
Scott & Katy Nimmons
Sherry Perry
Stephen Harding
Susan Carp

Susan Ernst
Theater Jones
Tim Perttula
Tony Thomson

<u>SUBSCRIBERS</u>

Andrew Wilensky
Audrey Golosky
Ben Nichols
Brandon Kennedy
Caroline West
Charles Dee Mitchell
Charlie Wilcox
Chris Mullikin
Courtney Sheedy
Damon Copeland
Daniel Kushner

Devin McComas
Evelyn Mizell
Hillary Richards
Johan Schepmans
John Darnielle
John Winkelman
Kyle Kubas
Lance Stack
Lesley Conzelman
Marisa Bhargava
Martha Gifford

Melanie Keedle
Michael Elliott
Michael Lighty
Neal Chuang
Ryan Todd
Samuel Herrera
Sandra Lambert
Shelby Vincent
Stephanie Barr
Steve Jansen
William Pate

THANK YOU ALL FOR YOUR SUPPORT.
WE DO THIS FOR YOU,
AND COULD NOT DO IT WITHOUT YOU.

MICHÈLE AUDIN · *One Hundred Twenty-One Days*
translated by Christiana Hills · FRANCE

BAE SUAH · *Recitation*
translated by Deborah Smith · SOUTH KOREA

EDUARDO BERTI · *The Imagined Land*
translated by Charlotte Coombe · ARGENTINA

CARMEN BOULLOSA · *Texas: The Great Theft* · *Before* · *Heavens on Earth*
translated by Samantha Schnee · Peter Bush · Shelby Vincent · MEXICO

Cleave, Sarah, ed. · *Banthology: Stories from Banned Nations* · IRAN, IRAQ, LIBYA,
SOMALIA, SUDAN, SYRIA & YEMEN

LEILA S. CHUDORI · *Home*
translated by John H. McGlynn · INDONESIA

ANANDA DEVI · *Eve Out of Her Ruins*
translated by Jeffrey Zuckerman · MAURITIUS

ALISA GANIEVA · *Bride and Groom* · *The Mountain and the Wall*
translated by Carol Apollonio · RUSSIA

ANNE GARRÉTA · *Sphinx* · *Not One Day*
translated by Emma Ramadan · FRANCE

JÓN GNARR · *The Indian* · *The Pirate* · *The Outlaw*
translated by Lytton Smith · ICELAND

NOEMI JAFFE · *What are the Blind Men Dreaming?*
translated by Julia Sanches & Ellen Elias–Bursac · BRAZIL

CLAUDIA SALAZAR JIMÉNEZ · *Blood of the Dawn*
translated by Elizabeth Bryer · PERU

JUNG YOUNG MOON · *Vaseline Buddha*
translated by Yewon Jung · SOUTH KOREA

JOSEFINE KLOUGART · *Of Darkness*
translated by Martin Aitken · DENMARK

YANICK LAHENS · *Moonbath*
translated by Emily Gogolak · HAITI

ÓFEIGUR SIGURÐSSON · *Öræfi: The Wasteland*
translated by Lytton Smith · ICELAND

SERHIY ZHADAN · *Voroshilovgrad*
translated by Reilly Costigan-Humes & Isaac Stackhouse Wheeler · UKRAINE

FORTHCOMING FROM DEEP VELLUM

GOETHE · *The Golden Goblet: Selected Poems*
translated by Zsuzsanna Ozsváth and Frederick Turner · GERMANY

JUNG YOUNG MOON · *Seven Samurai Swept Away in a River*
translated by Yewon Jung · SOUTH KOREA

DMITRY LIPSKEROV · *The Tool and the Butterflies*
translated by Reilly Costigan-Humes & Isaac Stackhouse Wheeler · RUSSIA

DOROTA MASŁOWSKA · *Honey, I Killed the Cats*
translated by Benjamin Paloff · POLAND

JESSICA SCHIEFAUER · *Girls Lost*
translated by Saskia Vogel · SWEDEN

KIM YIDEUM · *Blood Sisters*
translated by Ji yoon Lee · SOUTH KOREA

MATHILDE CLARK · *Lone Star*
translated from the Danish by Martin Aitken · DENMARK

ANNE GARRÉTA · *Dans l'beton*
translated from the French by Emma Ramadan · FRANCE

MÄRTA TIKKANEN · *The Love Story of the Century*
translated from Swedish by Stina Katchadourian · FINLAND